## The Urbana Free Library

To renew materials call
217-367-4057

INTERCOURSE

# INTERCOURSE

stories

**Robert Olen Butler**

**CHRONICLE BOOKS**
SAN FRANCISCO

Copyright © 2008 by Robert Olen Butler.
All rights reserved. No part of this book may be reproduced in
any form without written permission from the publisher.

This is a work of fiction. Names, places, characters, and incidents
are products of the author's imagination or are used fictionally.

Some of the stories in this book originally appeared in *Playboy,
Conjunctions, The Kenyon Review, The Virginia Quarterly
Review, Weber, New Letters, Vestal Review,* and on Nerve.com
and NarrativeMagazine.com.

Library of Congress Cataloging-in-Publication Data:
Butler, Robert Olen.
Intercourse : stories / by Robert Olen Butler.
    p. cm.

ISBN: 978-0-8118-6357-5

I. Title.
PS3552.U8278I58 2008
813'.54—dc22
                    2008012859

Manufactured in Canada

Designed by Brooke Johnson

10 9 8 7 6 5 4 3 2 1

Chronicle Books LLC
680 Second Street
San Francisco, California 94107

www.chroniclebooks.com

*for* my son, JOSHUA,
with my love and admiration

*—What were you thinking?*
*—When?*
*—During.*
*—During.*
*—Yes. Not what goes where. Thinking deep down.*
*—About you.*
*—Liar.*
*—So what were* you *thinking?*
*—About you.*

## ADAM

7, first man

## EVE

7, first woman, his wife

*on a patch of earth cleared of thorns and thistles, a little east of Eden, the first day after the new moon of the fourth month of the eighth year after Creation*

## ADAM

the dust of the ground rises around us as we move and clench and thrash, and the Creator's vast dark face fades and the woman grows slick and the dust turns to mud, and in the distance to the west I hear the trees stirring from a sweet breeze, but here the air is still, save for our breath, we are a great wind now ourselves, the two of us, we are rushing across the face of the earth and all that we left behind was good, but behold, naked is good too, and I named the animals one by one, the Creator brought them and I named them, and again I have some naming to do—of these parts of her I am seeing as if for the first time—but that will have to wait, I am a running river now and the names I already named will have to do: her two young fawns, her clam, her ass, which I ride

## EVE

I was happy but to tangle the holding parts and the walking parts and lie here quietly in the clean space he has made for us, but he is pawing and fondling and crying out and whimpering and perhaps that is good too, like when he took the apple from me, he was quiet then and he is boisterous now but it is the same: I offer and he takes, and I had nothing to give the Creator and all that He gave was for the man, and a shadow fell on the path and something was there and it came forth hissing prettily and he said *You're not stupid* and he was right and what he gave was sweet in me, but this man is not, he is flailing around and proud of his own little snake

## ZEUS, IN THE FORM OF A SWAN

982, King of the Gods


## LEDA

20, Queen of Sparta


*in an inner courtyard in the palace, Sparta, 1215 BC*

the swan was a mistake, these creatures who mate with just one, for now that I have her before me I am compelled to explain, though all I have are whoopings and trumpetings and undulant dippings of the head: I am married to my own sister—by Fate, by necessity, you understand—and she has her hair piled high on her head in a polos and she never lets it down and she is murderously jealous and worse, she goes every year to the spring at Kanathos and renews her virginity and I have to start all over again— anyone who desires a virgin is a fool—and you have to understand, my father hated me, he hated all his children, he ate them up at birth, swallowed them whole, and only because my mother gave a swaddled rock in my place did I escape their fate, and growing up I often thought it would have been better just to be eaten, for I spent all my young life dangling from a rope from a tree so that I was neither on the earth nor in the sky nor in the sea and thus invisible to the old man, but it has made the dangling part of my body the most treasured center of my being, you see, and so here I am, the king of the gods, making a fool of myself as a bird just to get under your gown

## LEDA

I knew who you were as soon as you flapped down from the moonlit sky and started whooping and trumpeting while my husband snored away inside the palace after emptying himself in me as if I were a fat temple sheep, and now it's you, with your wings quivering and your neck snaking around: if you wanted me so badly why is your breath reeking of barley, you had to turn yourself into a swan, fine, but you have such a passion for me that on your way you had to take time to land in a field somewhere and play the swan eating the crops, and as soon as you're done here you'll be off scudding around on the river with some swan bitch dipping your heads deep under the dark water together sucking at weeds while I'm left with this lesser king and eggs to lay

# HELEN

25, Queen of Sparta, wife of Menelaus

# PARIS

22, Prince of Troy

*in a villa on the island of Cranae in the Laconian Gulf, 1194* BC

## PARIS

Cassandra pulled at her hair and proclaimed the fire I will bring to Troy along with my Helen, and at last she is right, my sister the seer, I burned at the first sight of Helen and now I am a raging tall-flamed pine fire at her touch and it will never stop, this hot billowing in me, even as she lies beneath me placid and cool as the snows of Mount Gargarus and her head falls back languidly to the side and her arm rises and her hand curls outward, the long fingers flaring as if to clutch some invisible thing, and I might as well not even be here, for her eyes are the blue of the Aegean and swimming deep inside them, far out of sight, are her goddess thoughts, perhaps of her father Zeus, who waits for her immortal body that one day will lie languidly upon a couch on Olympus when she will belong to the gods, but for now, in spite of her distraction, she is mine

## HELEN

he is older, my Menelaus, his arms are strong and he is a king, but too strong, but too much a king: what of the beauty of my face and my neck and my hands and my breasts and my thighs, what of all the heroes of Greece who came to woo me and I chose a man with strong arms who was soon to be a king, but then his vast shadow passed over my face, my body, and I vanished and he would not stand aside, and then a prince came, a young man who chose a gift from between three vying goddesses and he declined the power of a great warrior and he declined the wealth of kings and he chose instead the love of the most beautiful woman in the world, me, who for nine years has lived in a shadow, and so the prince and I have come down from his ship on this island, the spray of salt from the sea still on our eyelids, our lips, our throats, and we have rushed to a private chamber with cicadas singing outside our window and we taste the salt on each other and he is beautiful in face and neck and hands and chest and thighs, but not as beautiful as me

# HELEN

35, Princess of Troy

# MENELAUS

42, King of Sparta

*on board his ship in the Aegean Sea, after retrieving her at the end of the Trojan War, 1184 BC*

## MENELAUS

this is familiar, after a decade, this is too familiar, I should have just let her go, I should have spared the lives of so many of our warriors, but these are the bodies we men have been given to live in, these are the gods' gifts of sword and shield and knife and fist and teeth and the gifts of strategy and cunning and the gift of bravery to stand before the ferocity of your own imminent death and fight, and so if it had not been for this woman who is beneath me once again that we fought and died, it would have been for something else, in some other place, against some other foe, who, in their own warrior hearts, would have cared as little as we about the reason: it is what we do

## HELEN

the gift from the gods rolled heavily in amongst us, towering in the center of our city, a vast horse of pine with a beautiful head, nostrils flared, its mane erect, its flanks glittering with torchlight, and I understand that long before, Paris had become a fool and a coward, shooting arrows from the parapets and pawing at me in our own bed each night as if it were the first time while the heroes of Troy died beyond the walls using their swords, and I understand that my face is still beautiful, even this many years later, even night before last, even lit in the mirror by Troy in flames outside my bedroom window, and I understand the gods gave me the gift of my beauty and the gods gave Paris the gift of the most beautiful woman in the world, but deep within these gifts our own destruction crouched, biding its time

# MARY MAGDALENE

24, prostitute

# TIBERIUS AURELIUS GAVROS

22, Roman soldier

*beneath a fig tree just outside Capernaum on the Sea of Galilee,* AD 28

from a distance, from the shade of a tree where I stood watching him beside the well, he seemed important, the men around him seemed to wish to shrink near him, make themselves very small, they were eager for him to speak, and I thought to wait to find him alone and perhaps he would provide the pieces of money I need, which this Roman provides now instead, but that was another woman thinking those things, the same woman beneath this man now—she does not understand fully yet—even as some other woman, thinking these new thoughts, hovers a ways apart, up in the branches of this fig tree, looking off toward the town where I feel him waiting, for at the well his eyes turned to me, away from the men, I could see his eyes clearly, even from a distance, and they knew me

# TIBERIUS

now that I have killed a man, now that I have at last killed a man—a man who was crying against Rome and waving a knife in this barren place of dust and weeds and houses of crude basalt blocks stuffed with mud—now that the rest of my life has truly begun with the quickness of my hand on my gladius, its blade going in softly, easily, finding a spot between his ribs, now that I tremble inside cursing my birth to a father who is a centurion and has created me for this, now that I tremble for what my hands can so easily do, I touch this body beneath me with these same hands and beg them remember this moment when they feel hungry for gentleness, and I wish to thank her, thank her generosity: though I pay her, it is not enough for what she gives me

## CLEOPATRA VII

28, Queen of Egypt


## MARCUS ANTONIUS

42, general and member of Rome's ruling triumvirate



*on her royal barge in the River Cydnus at Tarsus,* AD *41*

the sound of flutes and harps and lyres and, in their pausing, the sound of water lapping at the barge and I am an ambitious man and I am a man of battle and my head always has sounds on its horizon—the clanging of swords and the grunting of men and even, to an ear attuned to it, the sucking sound of sword in flesh, and this sound is the same, inside me and out: that soft sucking sound, now beneath me, my mansword and the flesh of a queen, but these other sounds are in me, as well, of the music and of the river in this floating world, where she waited for me tonight amidst a thousand torches, beneath a golden canopy, the queen reclining on her couch draped in an azure peplos fallen off her shoulder to bare her breasts, her hair braided all about her head, she was the very vision of Venus, opening wide for Marcus Antonius, and I am an ambitious man and I can overcome Octavian and rule Rome and perhaps I will, but what higher ambition is there than to fuck a goddess and I might well choose to float on her river forever in peace   .

## CLEOPATRA

how simple it was, how nakedly alluring, me rolled into a carpet like the womb and I rolled out with no sounding of trumpets, no scuffle of subjects going prostrate, and with no perfumes or jewels or silks upon me but I rolled in a thin swaddling of linen as a newborn child onto the floor and the great Julius Caesar rose in surprise from his chair and my breasts had gone bare and my loins as well and I very slowly covered them and spun and folded my legs under me and I lifted my face to him and it began, and Caesar touched me quite gently—unlike this stone-fingered Antonius—and he gave me my throne over my brother, whom he had drowned in the Nile, and my sister, whom he had pursued into exiled refuge in the temple at Ephesus, and he took me to his Rome where he exalted me, and then he died on my behalf on the steps of the Forum, and now with riches and pomp and music it begins again, and though this one touches me roughly, it will do, and the first thing I will ask of him is that he kill my sister

# ATTILA

47, Khan of the Huns

# ILDICO

17, his twelfth wife

*in his bed in Pannonia, on their wedding night, as he simultaneously dies from ruptured esophageal varices,* AD 453

a sudden warmth deep in my throat like the bloom on the chest of an enemy as the arrow flies in and I cannot draw a breath and I lift up and try again and again and there is nothing but the old man, the Shaman of Rome, the Papa called Leo, and I am on horseback at the ford of the River Mincius and he comes on foot and I dismount because he wears golden robes and I know he carries invisible arrows, though I can still take his life, my hand moves to the hilt of the Sword of Mars, which came to me long ago as a sign of my greatness, and this man in gold pleads quietly that I do not press on from this place to his Rome to sack it and burn it and he says *Do not think that you deal simply with Valentinian, for my Emperor is not of this world* and I do not understand, but my hand wants to kill him at once and take his golden robe for spoil and I would advance on his city, but then another man appears, assembling himself from the empty air beside the Shaman, and my horse knows to mutter and rear and this man is lank and draped in linen and he has an uneven beard and dark quiet wounds in his side and he wears a crown of thorns and he advances, and though he carries no weapon I begin to tremble, and he says very softly *I am his Emperor* and he stops before me and he angles his head backward and to the side and he offers his naked throat, and I know that if I cut it I am lost

## ILDICO

I cannot stop my legs from shaking, my chest from trembling, even with the weight of him on me, and the root of every hair in my head burns from the ceremonial dragging to his bed, and outside, his warriors vibrate their tongues, filling the air with cries like birds of prey come to wait beyond this canopy of white linen, wait in the flicker of pine torch, wait until he is done with me to pick the flesh from my bones, and now he rears like a horse and gasps and gasps, though I can tell he is not finished inside me, and now he falls heavily upon me again and he grows still, and lo, he is suddenly weak, he is gentle suddenly, and a sweet hopeful surging comes into me, for I see there is a side to my fierce new husband that perhaps will let me hold him close, and I put my arms about him

# IZUMI SHIKIBU

29, lady of the court, poet

# PRINCE ATSUMICHI

31, nobleman of the court, poet, husband of Princess Atsumichi

*in Izumi's rooms in the King's North Palace, Kyoto, Japan, 1003*

## PRINCE ATSUMICHI

she looks at the moon
I see the same moon alone
her poem arrives:
wild geese fly in a night white
with moonlight pure as her heart

## IZUMI

what he gives is white
the sea calm then rising up
then coming to shore
the wave rushes and churns thick:
white of the moon, you are dull

## LUCREZIA BORGIA

21, daughter of Pope Alexander VI, Rodrigo Borgia

## ALFONSO D'ESTE

25, her husband, eldest son of the Duke of Ferrara

*in their bridal chamber at the Castello Estense, Ferrara, 1502*

## LUCREZIA

almost married to Valencia at age eleven, almost married to
Naples at twelve, married to Milan at thirteen, a man of twenty-
seven years with strong teeth and a limp member, and I wore
red velvet trimmed in ermine and woven with gold thread, and
when he was useless to the Borgia men—as he was to me—they
could have slit his throat and thrown him into the Tiber and I
would not have cried, but they simply annulled him and I was
married at seventeen to Naples, to Alfonso of Bisceglie, who was
seventeen, and we were one in mind and body as well as years
and his skin was smooth as Travertine marble and I wore black
velvet and I was a night sky of rubies and diamonds and I wore
a girdle of pearls and a diadem of chased gold, and when he was
useless to the Borgia men—though I loved him desperately still—
my brother had him stabbed and beaten and then my brother
strangled him to death with his own hands, and today I wore a
gown of gold with purple satin stripes and sleeves of ermine and
a cloak of ermine and I give my body now to Ferrara and he is
accustomed to whores and he is accustomed to artillery but he has
taken me away from Rome at last, far away, far from Rome at last,
and at last I no longer have to look at the face of my father, the
face of Christ's Church on earth, for my father took my body to
himself when I was eight and in the dark he whispered *You will
always be married to me*

## ALFONSO

it is whispered in certain places that she poisoned the last one, some boy, and it is whispered she nightly fucks her father on the altar of St. Peter and it is whispered she had his bastard son, a creature with horns and a cloven hoof they had to burn at the stake before the sunset of its first day, but my father says she is a crucial alliance with Rome and she is the city of Cento and the city of Pieve and the harbor of Cesenatico and she is a dowry of a hundred thousand ducats and for these things she is not a murderer and she is not a slut to her father, and I did not truly know what she was until I rode out to her procession a day early and caught her just arrived for the night at Castel Bentivoglio and she came to me in the courtyard brushing the road dust from her riding dress and her golden hair was falling about her shoulders and she surely was unhappy at my seeing her for the first time like this and she lifted her long face to me and her pale blue eyes fixed on me and she smiled a smile like the muzzle flash of a cannon and I took her hand and bent low to kiss it and she whispered *I am your wife* and I knew that she was

## HENRY VIII

44, King of England


## ANNE BOLEYN

34, Queen of England


*at the house of Sir William Sandys near Basingstoke, England, October 1535*

# HENRY

he conjures himself corporeal from the very air: imperious dark eyes and cropped auburn hair and a small mouth shaping kisses and pouts and commands and his shoulders are broad and his limbs are long and his fingertips flare above the vast dark ocean on one side and the wide cold sea on the other and he steps forward with first one foot upon the cliffs of Cornwall and then the other upon Dover and he bestrides the land and he looks out to the wide world beyond, my son, my sweet son, and as I am England now, he will be England then, and by the prickish essence I give yet again to this woman, I will be England once more. Or else

## ANNE

I alone made England's alliance with France and I lifted the worldly evils of the papacy from our peoples' religious life and I bestowed all the wisdom of Cromwell upon the king and I established the right of a commoner to become a noble by his own thoughts and deeds and I gave more alms to the poor of the land than any highborn in history, and it all comes to this: a bejeweled codpiece falls and from a slash in a pair of breeches comes a too-small prick attached to a fat and distracted man and if its fluids do not blend with mine such to create a boy, I will sure be cast aside, or worse, and all that I am, all that I ever can be, is my cunt

# WILLIAM SHAKESPEARE

29, poet and playwright

# HENRY WRIOTHESLEY,
# THIRD EARL OF SOUTHAMPTON

20, courtier and literary patron

*in Shakespeare's rooms in St. Helen's Bishopsgate, London, 1593*

proud Nature humbled by the work of its own hand: his azure eye, his auburn tress, the chest it hangs on white as the sun can seem when veiled in silken cloud, his silken doublet white as cloud cast off to bare the fire beneath, and if his heart be sun and his chest be sky then his eye be heaven and his earth below be forested lush around a great high oak that stands stripped clean of limbs from lightning strike: I give my limbs to this land and touch his beating heart and burn, and yet he is night as well as day, a well as well as tree, a well dug deep and dark and I send my vessel down: he is, in flesh, the world inconsonant made one: my young man, my dark lady

## HENRY

I soon will lie alone and he will cross the room and sit at his table and once again he will take up his goose quill and find it blunt and take up his knife and bend and squint and turn slightly to the light from the window and begin his sweet circumcision, playing at the tip with the blade, making it less blunt, then sharp, then sharper still, and he will pause and touch the tip to his tongue and he will pull the ink pot nearer to him and dip the pen, dip it deep, the tip growing wet and dark, and he will withdraw and let it drip and drip till it stops, and then he will bend to his paper and his words will come and the tiny scratch of his quill will shudder its way up my thighs and I am pen and I am ink and I am his words

# COTTON MATHER

56, clergyman and author


# LYDIA LEE MATHER

45, his third wife


*in their home in Boston, 1719*

## COTTON

O Heavenly Father, please let this madness lift from her, my sweet Consort, my temporal delight, my Wife, for I know she is merely mad, I acknowledge the errors of my youth when I spoke and wrote to condone the hunt for witches in Salem, the nineteen hanged and the four who died awaiting the gallows and the one pressed to death by stones all hover about my soul and, to their credit, mercifully hold their tongues, but I feel them there and I acknowledge my sins against them for they were at worst mad, and if one or two were what was feared, then it would have been better that those go free than that the innocently deranged, Your children in need, be persecuted, and You are teaching me still, O stern and loving Father: she hissed and she wailed and she threw an ink pot and she ripped my sermon and she stood trembling in the kitchen and cursed me and cursed the hearth and cursed the broom and cursed the veal and the butter and the pickled barberries and yet abruptly these paroxysms ended, as they always do, and then she humbled her body before me in tender entreaties and ardent praises and sweet pleadings for us to enact the meek and abject yielding that is her proper place in the world that You have created, and I beg You, O Heavenly Father, to forgive these worldly acts we presently perform and to transform them into a healing of her affliction

## LYDIA

O pudding, O pudding for my husband, O pudding I dance you, my pudding, I sing you, my pudding, for you are my life, my pudding of hog's liver, my Lord and husband's favorite, I will take a nice fat liver and I will work it in my hands for a time and I will parboil it and I will shred it small, very small, so it will soften sweetly and it will give forth its juices, and I will beat the pieces very fine in a mortar and mix them in my earthen pot with the thickest and sweetest cream and I will strain it and into the liver I will put six yolks of eggs and two whites of eggs and the grated crumbs of a penny whiteloaf and then currants and dates and cloves and mace and coarse-grain sugar and saffron and salt and an excellent swine suet, but before the boiling and before the laying of it all on the iron grid over the coals for broiling, when, my sweet pudding, you are still raw and redolent of organ and spices and blood, I will add a tittle of wormwood and a minim of henbane and the eye of a freshly killed newt

# WOLFGANG AMADEUS MOZART

31, composer

# NANCY STORACE

21, soprano

*in her rooms at the Hotel Belvedere in Vienna, after the premiere of his aria "Ch'io mi scordi di te," written for her, on the eve of her permanent departure to her home country of England, February 23, 1787*

## WOLFGANG

I leap onto her lap and into her arms and I am six years old and she is the Empress and I am a genius I am a miracle the fingers of my left hand are still tingling from the violin strings and they find first the rope of pearls along her waist and then the embedded diamonds upon her stomacher and the ruffle along her bodice and at last ever so delicately the flesh of her in the treble cleft of breasts and chest and as my hand moves I kiss her throat a long run of demisemiquaver kisses and I am but a little boy, she thinks, as she lifts my offending hand and kisses its palm and perhaps I am but I am a genius and her flesh smells of musk and upon it are the smells of orange blossom and sandalwood and rose and she laughs a trilling laugh and holds me close and later, beyond her sight and the Emperor's, I stand beside Maria Antonia Josefa Johanna von Habsburg-Lothringen their daughter and her eyes are an arpeggio of gray and blue and her lower lip is pouting all the time and we have counted it out that she is but eighty-six days older than me and I put my hand in hers and I begin to finger the Bach D-Minor Chaconne in her palm and she angles her head a little in my direction *I will marry you* I say but I did not and now my fingers fly upon soprano-flesh encoring my farewell to Nancy this night: I play the pianoforte upon her, modulating from the G minor of the recitative to the E-flat major of the aria, and though she fills the room with the trilling of her laughter I can hear her singing

## NANCY

I have filled my mouth with him, with his music, and I sing him even now in my head where my voice does not have to keep up, where I do not have to sing actual words, it is all *nota e parola*, every note a sound, and so I cling with an infant's babble to his back and we rise up and float out the window and we fly, as only composers can fly, on pure senses, just the sound itself, no words at all, no meanings, and I cling to him and his bones are fragile as a bird's and his heart beats fast as a bird's and we fly above Vienna and out into the mountains and I look higher into the night sky and my mind slows and the lights burn at the edge of the stage and I lift my face toward the Emperor in his gilded box and I sing actual words *Stelle barbare, stelle spietate* and I sing this now to the sky outside our window *Oh brutal stars, oh pitiless stars* in the morning I will leave this tiny man with the bad skin and his ravening restlessness and whose genius presently animates his hands upon me: your music is perfect, my little Wolfgangerl, but for this, there are too many notes

# LOUIS XVI

23, King of France


# MARIA ANTONIA JOSEFA JOHANNA VON HABSBURG-LOTHRINGEN, KNOWN IN FRANCE AS MARIE ANTOINETTE,

21, Queen of France


*for the first time, on the eve of their seventh wedding anniversary, in the royal bedroom at Versailles, May 15, 1777*

she doesn't like me smelling of coal fire from my forge where I have just repaired a beautiful old Beddington lock and she narrows her little pig eyes at me and pouts out even farther her Habsburg lower lip and her hair is poufed up high and appears to have tiny birds living in it along with their nest and parts of a tree, and her brother has arrived from Austria and is about to insult me, and if I were my father, if I actually wanted to be what I am, I would have this man's head cut off with a blunt ax after he walks me through the grounds of the Trianon and asks if my member is working properly, and now I must try to understand that this matter is about a key and a lock: her warded lock, full of hidden obstructions, cylinders and flat metal plates with tiny separations that must all be entered at precise angles and all at once, and my key must somehow fit, and perhaps it is true that the future of France depends on this thing I am now doing but I would much prefer to put my member in the forge until it is yellow-hot from the flame and then pound it on an anvil with a hammer

## MARIE

I turn my face away and angle my head down and against my shoulder and I try to smell myself and not the royal blacksmith who has somehow found his way to my bed in place of the king who vanished long ago, and I smell of jasmine and iris and orange blossom and tuberose and cedar and I am but a little girl and my mother the queen's own fingertip draws a cool line of scent behind my ear and now she and I are listening to a little boy playing his violin and even as his one hand moves quickly on the neck of his instrument and the other draws the bow slowly he lifts his eyes to me and they are blue-gray just like mine and now we are standing apart and I feel his hand slip into mine and he begins to touch me there: his fingers run about my palm as if I were his violin and he begins to hum a sweet soft tune so that only I can hear and I know he loves me and I think to lean over and kiss him but my mother looks my way from across the room and lifts her hand to call me to her and I do not kiss him, but now yes, but now yes, I turn my face and I lean close and I kiss my Wolfgang Amadeus on the cheek and I whisper *Marry me*

# THOMAS JEFFERSON

45, U.S. Ambassador to France

# SALLY HEMINGS

16, slave, half-sister to Jefferson's dead wife

*at his residence in the Hôtel de Langeac, Paris, 1788*

the last eight miles to my hilltop on horseback in deep snow, Patty throwing her head back to laugh, her breath pluming into the moonlight *How difficult it is to come home with you, Mr. Jefferson* and then the doorway is drifted high with the snow and I lift her into my arms to carry her through and the servants are asleep and the fires are out and we are home at last and I find a Château Latour and I start a fire and we drink and she turns her face to me *My husband* she says and there in our bedroom on our wedding night the firelight isn't enough to keep the night's darkness from tainting her face, like this face now, Sally's, her very blood shared with Patty, but her face darkened from within, as if through memory, as if by death, as if by my six-year grief, and Patty throws her head back at the run of her hands on the keys and I finger my strings lightly, the Bach sonata carrying us both and I am wooing still and she will say yes and we will marry and she will die, and I look into these eyes now and now and they are dark, Patty's hazel charred into deep blackness, but the shape of them is the same and I hear the Bach and I run now inside like Patty's hands running on her harpsichord I run and I run and I pursue my happiness

## SALLY

so easy to come to this at last: he is playing his violin and it is very sad, the music, and I stand for a long while quiet in the doorway, behind him, his shoulders hunched forward a little, his hair—I have enough of the blood of my father and my mama's father in me that I can blush in this color of his hair—he bears my blush, which I see on my cheeks in the mirror with the eagle near the parlor door when I turn my face at his passing—his hair catches the light from the fireplace and he draws his bow back and forth on his violin, his elbow rising and falling—and I move to him and he stops playing, he knows I am behind him, and he knows how fast my heart is beating, and he ceases playing and he turns to me and his eyes are so sad and I will never as long as I live know how I come to lift my hand and put it on my master's face but I do and I am happy

# NAPOLÉON BONAPARTE

26, general in command of the French "Army of Italy"

# JOSÉPHINE DE BEAUHARNAIS

33, his wife

# FORTUNÉ

4, pug, her dog

*at the Palazzo Serbelloni, Milan, in the midst of his invasion of Italy, their third night together in the 129 days of their marriage, July 13, 1796*

## JOSÉPHINE

O my darling my darling, in bed again with you my darling, we shall be in bed again soon, even as we fucked our way from Paris to Milan, O my lieutenant, my hussar, my sweet Hippolyte, from inn to inn and also from riverbank to meadow and even, with sublime alacrity, in the carriage while the entourage pissed behind trees, the new France does not understand its own military ranks: attend to the true insignia, ye Directors of the Republic, this lieutenant is far above this general and it is signified by neither gorget nor epaulets but by the length of their swords, though, my darling Hippolyte, I'm afraid you must share my love, share my bed, for sometimes it is necessary that love gently separate itself in two, and my other love breathes heavily now and I listen to him with sweet attention: he sat until a few moments ago at the foot of the bed watching, my sweet Fortuné, and I hear him still

## NAPOLÉON

consider the musket, our infantry's beloved Charleville, consider the musket ball and its speed from the muzzle, slow, in truth, climbing quickly and falling quickly, as well, aim carefully, my men, at the head from two hundred meters, at the waist from a hundred, at the knees from fifty, so for my wife, who took her blatant neglectful time joining her triumphant husband, I ponder a near shot, aiming at her shins and plugging her in her woman-hood, and as for this wretched animal she insists on having in our bed, I will put the muzzle in its mouth so there is no doubt, but now, but wait, ah my wife, my ravishing Joséphine, she banishes these thoughts at once by touching the back of my thigh, clasping me there with her befurred womanhood: and yet how can that be, for she is below me

## FORTUNÉ

big dog on my doggie and I missed her signifying or I'd've been there first, but itchy itchy now and I niggle my claw into my side and that's very good, and I could just keep doing this, I suppose, till my doggie is done with the big stinky slick dog, niggle niggle at my side, but now the itchy is gone and I stop, a little regretful, for that was a nice itchy-niggly, and my tongue is cool, flopping in the air, and there's something gathering in my nose and another itchy begins down in my snozzle, and I wonder if I need to do some licking there, but no, snozzle has its own uppity uppity ideas now, and my doggie is occupied but, surprisingly, since it's sickly slick, there's suddenly a certain je ne sais quoi about the big dog, and I hop on

# BENJAMIN

23, field slave

# HANNAH

17, house slave

*in his slave quarters, Adams County, Mississippi, 1855*

## BENJAMIN

the bells going now in the middle of the night and the dogs' barking getting farther off toward the river and they say Jacob done run off and I seed him take the bullwhip today and I seed his face and I knowed he was up to running at last and the whip fire on my own back make me hold her on our sides and she is here, from the house she all the sudden here, and Jacob done give us this moment, in all the fuss she come to me and for God's sake she be soft along my thighs and on my belly and she be soft against my chest and she be soft upon my manhood and she be putting her soft mouth on mine and I am about to weep like the little nigger boy I used to be cause this is all so sweet and soft

## HANNAH

hold tight my Ben my Ben for the first time my Ben my Ben: you
go ahead make a sound now please, you don't have to do quiet,
there be plenty of uproar outside so you make a sound that can
take Master's voice away from my head *Come here girl come here*
and it's even bright morning sun and it's even his own parlor and
it's even his wife's stuffed couch and it's her antimacassar I am
clutching hard crumpling in the palm of my hand while he be
doing that thing and I be looking off to the sun out the window
and I wants to keep looking till I can go blind but I look away
cause I think of that man I seed out the window yesterday who
sees me and I make it in my head he be mine someday and I want
to have eyes to see him, and now there ain't no sun and there be
just pine board and a corn-shuck mattress and he doing close upon
me and now he do make a sound, a small one, something like the
sound you make holding back your voice when you is whipped,
but it's okay, my Ben, that sound'll do

JOHN WILKES BOOTH

24, actor


CATHERINE WINSLOW

26, actress


*in his rooms at the National Hotel, Washington, DC, after the opening of his production of* Richard III, *which was attended by President and Mrs. Abraham Lincoln, April 11, 1863*

## JOHN

you dare to watch even this, I look over my shoulder and there you are, sitting across the room, spindleleg crossed over spindleleg, cheeks sunk deep, sucked dry, as you are, of the last dewdrop trace of humanity, and you watch me in this bed even as you watched me tonight from your box: be gone, tyrant, be gone, don't you understand when I, as the villainous Richard, crawled on my belly like a snake on Bosworth Field, it was you I portrayed, it was you in my mind and in my body, and I regret this for Richard's sake, regret that I sensed you there watching and, in doing so, envenomed my Richard into a creature far more vile than he was—what were his sins compared to yours? your hobnailed boot pressed on the throat of a nascent nation, and even in my own Maryland, unconfederated still, you jail us without warrant, intercept our mail, persecute us for speaking our minds—and I grind now at Kate, my sweet Kate, my long-limbed Kate, she is Juliet above, on a balcony, combing her hair *She speaks yet she says nothing, what of that? her eye discourses, I will answer it* and I do, thrust by thrust, thrust by deep thrust, as deep as I would plunge a knife into a chest or fire a bullet into a brain, even as you clear your throat across the room

## CATHERINE

I saw what you thought no one saw, in your delicacy, the poor fool of a local actor in Chattanooga taken on at the last moment to play Montague and not merely forgetting his lines with you but swirling them up in some perverse new order which only made you look bad to a full house, and in the wings you put your arm around the man and I drew near, behind you, to hear you say, quite softly *Don't worry, my friend, you'll do better tomorrow* and the man wept on your shoulder, grateful, I'm sure, that you had not murdered him, which actors of only half your fame would be inclined to do, my sweet Wilkes, and oh how your Romeo tossed me around in passion, more Walt Whitman than William Shakespeare, my wild Wilkes, and always the grand grabbing and lifting and swooping would end with some grace note of your gentleness, a fingertip trailing across my wrist, the softest touch of your lips, a low word or two below your breath, that secret tender heart of yours: *My sweet Kate I see you clearly* and you do, and though you drive deep into me now such as to make my teeth rattle, I see your gentle eyes flash as I have not seen them before, flash with a dark loving fire for me

# ABRAHAM LINCOLN

54, President of the United States

# MARY TODD LINCOLN

44, First Lady

*in their bedroom on the second floor of the White House, Washington, DC, after attending the opening night of* Richard III, *starring John Wilkes Booth, April 11, 1863*

she rail-split my log long ago, the products of which were dispatched to erect a fence in some far land and leaving nothing erectable behind, but tonight my Mary wants this again after such a long while and what she needs is far above my poor power to add or detract, so I try to see her once more across the dance floor at the General Assembly ball, and her cousin Major Stuart has her by the elbow and is guiding her my way and her eyes are certainly blue, even from a distance, and her chestnut ringlets of hair quake above a great expanse of an exposed bosom that has been much admired all around already, I am fully aware, and she has not yet shrieked at me, indeed, in that moment as she draws near, has not yet spoken a single word to her future husband, though now, in this bed, she will soon speak at my slowness to respond, shriek, in fact, so let us strive on to finish the work we are in, and I do, I turn to look in another direction, my leg crossed, my hands on the arms of my chair, I look to the bright glow of the stage below me, just a few hours ago, and his face turns up and his eyes are as black as a cougar's come upon on a moonless night, and like the cougar's they burn, and if a cougar can purr, which being a cat, surely it can, this is its sound, the voice of this man before me: *Grim-visaged war hath smoothed his wrinkled front, and now, instead of mounting barbed steeds to fright the souls of fearful adversaries, he capers nimbly in a lady's chamber to the lascivious pleasing of a lute*: and his *lascivious pleasing* sighs its sibilance through my loins, even now, and I stir

when Richard III began to crawl on his belly like a snake crying
for a horse in vain, I knew the President would die, and soon, but
I am a brave woman and so I did not throw myself headfirst from
the box, I went on instead with my hands folded in my lap, with
my eyes holding steady on this actor, who was ludicrously beautiful as the ugly king, and I waited for this house and this bed
before I would myself cry out, from my fear, but now the cries do
not come and all I want is this man once more inside me, a last
time inside me, and would that tonight's beautiful actor could
play this ugly king, but Abe will do, Abe will have to do, Abe I
suppose, is necessary in this surprising desire, except Abe will not
do, he is slack and slow and so there is nothing to be done about
the knife or the bullet or the bomb, there is nothing to do about
this man's distaste for me, and words begin to boil up in my
bosom and I try to see him standing beside me in the parlor of
my sister's house and Reverend Dresser is before us in canonical
white and his brow is furrowed with God's serious purpose and
Abe is absolutely still, not a twitch, the ring, I know, in his hand,
engraved *Love Is Eternal*, and I am in white muslin and it's raining outside, raining hard, and I let the back of my hand touch
his, and suddenly now he has caught up and there is a touch, now
and now, and he is my husband and he is the President and we
both shall soon die

# MARTHA JANE "CALAMITY JANE" CANARY

24, frontierswoman

# JAMES BUTLER "WILD BILL" HICKOK

39, gambler and gunfighter

*in a back room at E. A. Swearingen's Cricket Saloon, July 31, 1876*

## JANE

he's been losing at poker and drinking himself almost to blind-
ness but not quite, I got him away first and I know he can still see
out of those pale blue eyes and it's me he's seeing and I reined in
my own jag so I could do this and remember it later, if anything's
been worth doing in my life it's Wild Bill and me in this bed right
now and it's been brewing since Fort Laramie and the trail to the
Black Hills where he could see firsthand how I could do with a
team of mules—bullwhacking better than any man—and I killed
a coyote from a hundred yards with an 1860 Colt Army pistol
while all the men were missing with rifles and he could see this,
my Bill, he could see with his own eyes, and even though it finally
took a goddamn dress and a goddamn bath and me hanging on
his arm like a white-slave girl afraid for her life, he's mine now
and he's looking me straight and true in the eyes while I go at
him and I can hardly see him for my own goddamn girl's tears
because I know this is never going to happen again

## BILL

I think I'm dead I think I'm dead and I can smell the flames of perdition already and I'm getting a little hot around the edges and it's begun, but they got to bury me first and some damn fool is acting like she don't even know how to lay a man into his coffin, give me back my goddamn clothes you ain't gonna bury me in the raw and they don't stuff you with anything in Deadwood but lead so just put my duds back on and leave me alone 'cause I'm a goner and I'm about to start weeping like a girl for some thing or other but what goddamn good was it all anyway, I think I'll just weep for my pair of sweet Colt 1851 Navy thirty-sixes with that cool slick ivory on my palms and the hammers cocked at the tips of my thumbs and then them barking away straight and true and no man could stand fair and square before me like that and live, and I wonder how they got me, probably from behind

WALT WHITMAN

64, poet

OSCAR WILDE

28, poet and playwright

*in Whitman's bedroom in his brother's house on Stevens Street in Camden, New Jersey, 1883*

## WALT

for this poet I sing, for this large boy, who cast off black velvet
coat, cast off pink cravat, cast off white silk shirt, cast off salmon-
colored stockings—O thou legs of many legs! not cast off the
stockings so much as carefully peeled each and shook it out and
draped it so as not to make it run—and he presents eyes now gray
now pale blue, jaw pendulous, lips tumescent, fingers long and
fondling, and he is not farmer, not ship joiner, not sawyer, not
mule skinner, not coal miner or fireman or hog reeve or hawker
or lamplighter—perhaps lamplighter, with my lamp only, whose
wick he puts to flame—not butcher or cobbler or cook but poet
but young but beautiful, my beard is white my skin is coarse my
one arm and one leg are weak still, from their stoppage long ago,
and they will stop again soon, leg and arm and belly and man-
root and heart and mouth, but for now I sing

## OSCAR

your body is not electric, my captain, it is not even a steam engine, it is a wood fire in an open field—I will say on Hampstead Heath, it is bad enough to think of the outdoors, so I will at least imagine your embers within the London city limits—but this room of yours, my dearest Walt, if only books and newspapers and foolscap were made of porcelain and pewter and cloisonné you would still have a distressing jumble of an antique shop but at least one could take a breath and handle an object or two, though do not mistake me, dear old man, I am not ungrateful as I touch you—every pubic inch of space is a miracle—we share so much, for out in the world they speak and write of us viciously, but contempt breeds familiarity and how sad it would be to make such grand gestures as we do make and not have the wide world to witness them, though this private gesture is, for the moment, the grandest of all, my sweet barbarian, your beard smells not of trees but of book paper and we are one: I sound my nuanced yip in the parlors of the world

## SIGMUND FREUD

42, psychiatrist


## MINNA BERNAYS

33, his sister-in-law


*in room 11 at the Schweizerhaus, Maloja, in the Swiss Alps, before sunrise, August 14, 1898*

only a few minutes ago in a dream I flew out this window and into the dark of the night and I was high above the rooftops of Maloja and before me I could see one isolated mountain rising from the Alps, tall and white in the moonlight, and I flew toward it faster and faster and then I was upon it, clinging to the merest bits of rock on its vast side, and above somewhere was a bird's nest and I had to go there, I began to climb the mountain and above me I could hear the mother bird in the nest—the loving mama bird—and I knew she was feeding two of her children—two female birds—and I was driven to climb faster and faster—I had to find the mother bird—I realized she would die unless I could find her quickly and put my hand upon her—and I climbed even faster, breathlessly, and at last I reached a ledge and I lifted my head and in front of me was the nest, wide and deep, and sitting inside were three birds—three plump, gray-feathered, long-beaked female birds—and they turned their heads to look at me and, as young birds of a certain age often are, the two girlchicks were indistinguishable from the mother bird—all three birds were identical and I had no way to sort them out, but I had to reach in and touch the mother in her nest or she would die: I looked at the three birds, the three birds looked at me, and then suddenly it was all right, suddenly it didn't matter, any of them would do: so here I am fucking my mother

## MINNA

I was very small and the room was very quiet for he had stopped breathing, my Papa, and then the room was full of my mother's sobbing, but what I noticed most was the smell of cigar smoke, the room was hazy with smoke, he'd had a last smoke before dying, he'd drawn into himself the smoke that I later understood helped kill him and then he'd breathed it back into the room and it hung in the air all about me, the smoke from his ravaged lungs hung all around and I knew he'd left me, I knew Papa had left me, and Ignaz my betrothed came home from Oxford and he lay in his room coughing and bleeding from the lungs and I stood in the doorway and he waved me away, perhaps for my sake, and he coughed and coughed again and then he left me also, and even when he is naked, Sigmund smells like cigars and he coughs a nasty rattling cough, but I know how I have done this, I know why I can tolerate loving him: because when he leaves, it won't be me he's leaving, it'll just be my sister

# LIZZIE ANDREW BORDEN

44, murderer, acquitted in 1892

# NANCE O'NEIL

30, actress

*in O'Neil's home, Brindley Farm, Tyngsboro, Massachusetts, 1904*

# LIZZIE

her hands the hands of Lady Macbeth that first time I saw her at the Colonial in Boston, she stands in a bright spot of light, her crimson hands flaring delicately before her, her eyes aflame at the only man in her world because he is a coward, and her vast, trilling voice fills me *A little water clears us of this deed* and I stand for a long while before him as he sleeps in the sitting room on the mohair sofa in his morning coat, his feet on the floor, and he is snoring, this man whose name I bear, whose touch I bear, my Papa, and the stepmother is finished already, upstairs, and the short-handled ax is light in my hand and I wait upon myself to decide: he gave away our farm in Swansea to the dead cow upstairs and he gave away the house on Fourth Street to her sister, and though to do all that would never have occurred to him on his own, he could not resist, he is a coward, and now Lady Macbeth pulls me close: a little of her wetness clears me of this deed from a poisonous heaven I want nothing to do with or from a hell in what may secretly be a just universe, look upon your daughter now, Father, look upon my nakedness and Lizzie Borden's and pound your chest in shame as you did with me trapped in the middle of a packed pew where you placed me so you could cry out my evil to heaven and the congregation *She goes off to a life in the theater and thereafter to an eternity in hell* and I tried once more with you, my bag was packed and I was looking beautiful— I could see myself in the foyer mirror and I trembled at myself and wanted you to tremble too—and you cried *Get thee behind me* but Lizzie would know what to do with you, Father, she would know: your hands are as hard as ax heads, Lizzie, your hands are as hot as blood, your hands have spots upon them, sweet Lizzie, just rub them clean on me

## JAMES JOYCE

24, writer

## NORA BARNACLE

22, his wife

*in their apartment on the Via Giovanni Boccaccio, Trieste,*
*May 23, 1906*

in the midst she's suddenly ghosteyed and boyfingered and she's gone away from me: who's that knocking at my door? a semen-sappy boy soprano singing *It's only me from over the sea, I'm Barnacle's Mike the sailor* and in he comes from his grave and he's ready to rollick her all over and he's barely had a chance to elbow Jim to the side in his own bed when I am moved to cry *Who the lungbloody hell is knocking up my door this time?* to which, in gasworky tenor, comes *It's only me from over the sea, I'm Barnacle's Mike the sailor* and sailor Mike the First, otherwise known as her girlhoodlove Saint Michael the Typhoided, having horned in, now horns out, and we slide away together side-by-hornied-side and press against the wall and sailor Mike the Second, otherwise known as her girlhoodlove Saint Michael the Consumptive, enters in from his grave and he sits beside us and we are trinitized before the flail of her and I implore them both to neither Nora burrower nor a Nora bender be, but I am the Madeflesh here and I've got God and the Holy Ghost on either side of me and how do I ever find frigging peace without having to die first

## NORA

I can hear his voice clear as can be and he's singing and it's August hot all around and it's dark but I am sitting still in my seat at the Antient Concert Rooms and he's in the bright lights onstage and John McCormack the Great is upcoming to sing but he sings first, my Jim, and it's the Croppy Boy confessing to a priest that he's going to fight for Ireland and the priest is a yeoman captain in disguise who jails him and murders him and I listen and I play the part of the croppy boy though it's me in my girl body and it's Jim that's hiding in priest's clothes and not knowing it's him I confess my lust for him since I'm after slipping my hands down his trousers when early we went walking and Jimmy was getting all jammy in my fingers and he sings so sweet so much sweeter than anyone could possibly sing even John McCormack and I'm still confessing to Father James and then he throws off his vestments and he jimmies me open and I'm trying to sit still in my seat his voice is so sweet and in my head he jims me full to bursting and though the concert room is deep summer hot my body shivers cold with joy as if there was snow falling all around

## PABLO PICASSO

24, artist

## FERNANDE OLIVIER

25, model

*on the forest floor on the slopes of Pedraforca in Catalonia, Spain, July 1906*

the chase through the trees her naked body flashing in sunlight her skin Yellow Ochre lightened only a little, a stand of downy oaks their foreground barks Cobalt Black cut and cut by Lead White, the trunks going darker as they recede into the shadows all around, the shadows black from Ultramarine and Rose Madder and a little Viridian to take out the purple, a black that has not forgotten the sunlight but where the Iberian wolves can live, and she is laughing and I catch her up and we fall and she rolls away, her body growing dark from the forest floor and my palette turns simple: it is the carbon black of charred bones of a cave-mouth fire and the flat yellows and browns and reds of the earth itself mixed with animal fat and I paint her on rock like an ancient beast with a thin stroke of black going into her to bring her down and there is a rushing in me and my hands are restless my hands are ravenous they move and with the fire-blackened stump of a wood shard I bring a wolf from the forest and it rages into her and rips her body apart beneath me and I paint in her blood, heavy and hard, impasto layer on layer, the Alizarin Crimson pure, my brush slashing like the teeth of the beast

## FERNANDE

in the first moments I was wet through with an August rain and he blocked my way into the Bateau-Lavoir though it seemed I could just rush over him he was such a small thing and he had a wet kitten tucked into the crook of his arm and I was living where I was living having escaped the fists of a father and a shop-clerk husband and then a sculptor and yet I could be alone in this strange warren of artists and I could be naked with them and they would be across the room and I could just sit and hold very still and this was a small obstacle, this man, until the few moments after the first moments when I looked into his eyes and no layer-after-layer of Cobalt Black could put the darkness of his eyes on canvas and yet—and yet—he held up this kitten mewing in his hands and he said in terrible French that he was its savior and I knew he was and I began to purr

## GERTRUDE STEIN

36, writer

## ALICE B. TOKLAS

33, her companion

*in their apartment at 27 rue de Fleurus, Paris, 1910*

## GERTRUDE

I touch her black wisp of a mustache the bottom edge of her black mustache just above her lip, certainly it is her mustache certainly it is hers the black mustache is hers certainly I touch her wisp of a mustache certainly with my fingertip along her lip certainly it is her lip certainly I touch above her lip I draw my fingertip along her black mustache above her lip I draw with my fingertip along her mustache from left mustache to middle indent along her mustache to right mustache and to middle indent and to left I draw my fingertip along her black wisp of a mustache: a melody, a shadow, an antimacassar, a white stain is wet weather is wet whether or not my fingertip draws a line that my fingertip draws along her mustache: this is this, this is certainly this mustache: her mustache is her mustache is her mustache

## ALICE

only done a few minutes ago typing upon her large novel on the big black Smith Premier in the atelier from the sheets of foolscap she wrote in the night that fall beside the desk as I type like leaves from a white tree and my fingers are slim and quick and they can do this thing for her whose hands are heavy with man muscle and whose fingers are plump and not suited to this work and for her also I sat with Madame Matisse this morning and spoke of the weather and the fashions and the vegetables while the husband spoke of genius with my Lovey in another room and I am happy to do this for her whenever a genius shows up with his woman, Madame Braque and Madame Gris and Picasso's Fernande and all the rest, and in the other room my Lovey is the plumpest manmuscled genius of any of them and when she touches me she is more man than woman the most man of any woman the most woman the most womanman the most woman who is a man who is a woman and she is both and both is she and both is so much better

# VICTOR DE SATODE PEÑASCO Y CASTELLANA

18, of independent means from Madrid

# MARIA JOSEFA PEREDEZE SOTO Y VALLEJO PEÑASCO Y CASTELLANA

17, his newly wed wife

*in their first-class cabin, C-65, on the RMS* Titanic, *near midnight, April 14, 1912*

## VICTOR

Señor John Jacob Astor smiled at me, he came into the first-class
dining saloon from the private party in the à la carte restaurant
and it was time for cigars and he was speaking to an older man
whose name I did not know and then he looked across at me and
then at my wife and then back to me and he smiled, one gentle-
man to another, one man to another, the two men with the most
beautiful wives on the ship—his as young as mine, which made
the smile even better, wiping away the years between us, we were
simply two men who know what this sweetness is—and tomorrow I will stay for the cigars and I will approach him and we will
smile and we will smoke a Fernández Garcia together, man to
man, but tonight it is not man to man, I am married to the most
beautiful woman on this great ship and I carried her to the room
so she would know she is mine forever as her father promised,
and now we are together and I feel her tremble at my touch and
as if by magic the whole room trembles with her

## MARIA

at the bottom landing of the Grand Staircase he swept me into his arms without a word and we looked each other in the eyes— we had seen each other's faces for such a little time—our true faces and not just photographs, not just the faces we put on sitting twice in my parents' parlor—and I did not know Victor de Satode Peñasco y Castellana to be a man who would lift me as easily as a goose-down pillow and to hold me close, but he is such a man, and he began to climb and I threw my head back into the nighttime sunlight of electric lights and we climbed and a bronze cherub appeared holding a lamp and this was our floor, only one above the dining room, and I whispered *Higher* and he carried me up to another landing and another until all I could see were the lights in the vast dome right above me and when we reached the top of the staircase I realized that we are married also for love, and I am breathless now with him upon me and all at once I tremble, but it is not from within me, something has happened

# MATA HARI

37, exotic dancer and courtesan

# JACK JOHNSON

35, world heavyweight boxing champion

*in a room at the Hotel Friedrichshof, Berlin, during Johnson's exile from the United States, 1913*

## MATA HARI

I dance: I dance for Shiva I dance to ask Shiva to destroy me once more I am Mata Hari born of a temple dancer who died at my birth and I was but thirteen when I myself first danced naked for Shiva at the temple but Shiva destroys me and remakes me yet again and I am Princess Anuba sending her lover to the bottom of the sea and he returns savaged by sea monsters and dying but he has in his bloody hand my heart's desire, the sacred black pearl, and the black pearl has become a man and has entered now into Anuba and I take him and he is part of me and Shiva destroys me as I dance once more, I am the temple smoke and I am the sea and I am the falling veils and I am my naked body, and what I am not is Margaretha Geertruida Zelle, and I am not a Dutch wife to a man who beats me, and I am not the mother of a son poisoned to death in Java by the husband of my husband's lover, I am not, I am dead, I am destroyed and I live again

## JACK

the tenor is in my head and he is singing sweet, this trouba-
dour, this wanderer with no place in the world, and he knows
how things be and he sings *Deserto sulla terra, col rio destino in
guerra*—I heard him a dozen times in Paris—and I got the words
up now in English and I can see myself back a few years in Reno
and James J. Jeffries and me is waiting to start and the crowd is
chanting *Kill the nigger* and the band is playing *All Coons Look
Alike to Me* and then suddenly I step forward before the bell, I go
out in the center of the ring and I start to sing in a voice so loud
they all shut the hell up and they listen and I sing *All alone on
the earth, I'll go forty-five rounds with my evil fate* and they don't
make another sound till I'm done and I only need fifteen of those
rounds and I'm still the champ, and so is Mister Verdi, me and
him are the heavyweight champs of the world

# GEORGE HERMAN "BABE" RUTH

21, baseball player

# JOSEPHINE RUGGLES

24, prostitute

*in the Chambre Rouge at Lulu White's all-octoroon Mahogany Hall,
Storyville, New Orleans, 1916*

## BABE

a bat in my hands a hickory bat long and heavy and the color of tobacco spit and I'm about to hit my first one and it's little Jack Warhop on the mound throwing his rise ball and it's the third inning in the Polo Grounds, and say but I'm swell at last, it's fine for me as a pitcher breaking off curves on the corner of the plate, but try to slip one by me with my bat in my hand and see what I can do, and here I am now in a fancy bed with a girl and she might as well see it all, she might as well see what I can do, and the same for all you girls in all the fancy rooms and in all the cheap cribs in Storyville, I'm out of the goddamn boy's home at last, out of St. Mary's, through being an orphan with two parents working a tavern across town, and now Mom's dead for real, and little Jack is standing sixty feet away and this is how you get it all back: your feet close together and your right shoulder swung around to him and the bat sitting easy on your left shoulder nuzzled in the crook of your neck and he winds and throws, and his rise ball is what he's got that says I don't belong where I am, and I can see the ball spinning, I can count the stitches, and what I do starts in my stomach, it starts in the center of me right there and it flows easy into my arms and hips and legs and I hitch back and glide on through and the groove is there and it's sweeter than any pussy, me passing into this invisible place, and there's a little push against the bat and a swell chunking sound and the ball is rushing off and up and up and it flies fast and far and farther still and it falls into the straw hats deep in the right-field stands and it's my first home run and I am still feeling its kiss, it kissed me hard and wet right on my bat

## JOSEPHINE

he yawps and grunts, this overgrown boy, and of a sudden he cries
*Say but I'm swell* and now is off to whooping again, but you're
not that swell I can tell you and I just try to hear beyond him,
the piano trickling up from the parlor downstairs, Lulu has let
a colored boy in tonight to play and he's doing it fine and they're
down there dancing the ragtime one-step on the parquet floor, not
the mudbuggers like this boy but the Americans from Uptown in
evening clothes, and I could be doing it with them, doing what
I really do: pulling the arm of a true swell around my waist and
facing him a little off center and taking his left hand in my right
and finding that easy-glide spot—our hands just a bit away from
us and a little up from the waist, my right elbow slightly bent,
my left hand cupping behind his right shoulder, my back straight
upright, my heels together and my toes turned outward, perfect,
like finding the lay of me in bed when I'm finally alone and can
sleep—and tonight we'll do the Castle Walk so I go up onto the
balls of my feet and stiffen my legs and I pull ever so slightly with
my palm behind his shoulder and with the tips of my fingers at
the back of his hand and he doesn't even know I'm leading and
we're off, stepping away long and smooth and quick around and
around Lulu White's whorehouse parlor and nobody does the
one-step like Jo and it's all for free

ERNEST HEMINGWAY

23, writer


CÉLINE GAUTHIER

34, prostitute


*in a brothel on the rue de la Huchette upon Hemingway's return to Paris to confirm that his wife, Hadley, had indeed lost virtually all of his manuscripts, including carbon copies, on a train, December 4, 1922*

## ERNEST

how did it begin, the one I ache for the most:

*We waited in the woods in the shadows of the trees the color of*

*They told us to stop the Germans from crossing the bridge and we waited in the woods. The shadows were*

*The shadows of the trees were gray. There were barrage balloons in the sky*

*We waited for the Germans while the barrage balloons floated over the Austrian lines*

*We waited in the woods and the shadows were the color of*

*We waited in the woods. The color of the shadows was gray*

*We waited in the woods for the Germans*

*The shadows*

*We waited in the woods for the Germans. The shadows of the trees were the color of gun metal. The barrage balloons*

*We waited in the woods for the Germans to try to cross the stone bridge. The shadows of the trees were the color of gun metal. Against the distant mountains we could see the barrage balloons floating over the Austrian lines. I felt I was already dead because she put every word I'd ever written into a valise and then lost it on a fucking train*

## CÉLINE

I wait and later I will go to the café and I will sit in the corner table, I will drink a calvados slowly, keeping my palms on the tabletop, my hands will rest on the coolness of the slate tabletop and I will watch Bernard behind the zinc bar, he will wipe the top of the bar lightly in long elegant strokes, in the long mirror behind the bar I will look at the bald spot on the back of his head, I know how the spot has grown since I first came to this restaurant and the zinc bar has grown darker, from a dark gray to nearly black, and I will not see myself in the mirror from the table where I sit, everything else is in the mirror but I am not, the calvados will taste of apples and a little bit of pear and I will drink it slowly and there will be nothing in my mind, the nothing of the tabletop and the nothing of the zinc bar and the nothing of the bare spot on Bernard's head and the nothing of the trees silhouetted outside against the electric light and the nothing of sitting very still and drinking slowly

JOSEPHINE BAKER

19, dancer


GEORGES SIMENON

22, writer


*in her rooms at the Hôtel Fournet, Montmartre, Paris, January 1926*

## GEORGES

oo la la la la la la la the butt, the most famous butt in Paris, sweetly compliant now, silent, but redolent of its fame onstage: this butt can laugh, this butt can sing, this butt can carry on a sublime dialog within its twinned self in its own language, one cheek quivering and then the other: *I am so beautiful my sister* yes yes I am too my sister *this city is watching us entranced and we are both so beautiful* we are and we are so chic wearing flamingo feathers or bananas as if they were a Paul Poiret or a Jean Patou we are so very chic *but we are even more beautiful utterly naked for we are the perfection of curves* ah yes we are the globes to the angles in art deco *it's true sister we are modern but we are also savage we are also primitive we are the jungle we are the night we are the call of birds*—wait, wait, what has Josephine done to her Georges—I am a man of words, nineteen novels already, full of elegant and simple words, and yet in praise I have just had her butt make bird calls: I have gone mad

## JOSEPHINE

oo la la how they want me to be blacker and blacker, even Georges, his pipe on the bed stand and his hands all over my naked butt and I just have to make my cheeks tremble there and he will cry out in French as wildly as Genevieve and she will answer from across the room in Monkey, but I keep them both quiet tonight, I am myself quiet inside and I cannot stop my mind, for tonight I danced as I always dance—some Charleston some Black Bottom, some Mess Around and Tack Annie and Shim Sham Break and some things I tell myself are Africa but are St. Louis, for all that, are me just knocking my knees and camel-walking and vibrating my butt and flailing my arms and legs—I danced as always but at the same time I was somewhere up in the balcony with these ravenous French watching me dance, which is something I almost never do, but just because I dance in a trance most of the time don't mean the dance has anything to do with what I am and what I am driven to want, which is something I got from St. Louis, as well: my hair is conked flat and lacquered, which the French don't understand the mean-ing of, and at the end I cross my eyes at them and I flap my arms like a backyard chicken, and they don't understand that either, but after it's all over and the night is gone and the sun comes up in Paris, each morning I get into my hotel bathtub and I soak in hot water and goat's milk and lemon and honey and Eau de Javel that they scour their sinks with and I soak and I soak till my pussy's on fire just so I can be white

## JEAN-PAUL SARTRE

24, recent graduate in philosophy from the École Normale
Supérieure

## SIMONE DE BEAUVOIR

21, recent graduate in philosophy from the Sorbonne

*in her fifth-floor rented room at 91 avenue Denfert-Rochereau,
Montparnasse, Paris, 1929*

too much of her too much silk skin, brick nipple, face of porcelain, too much of this room too much cane chair and claw-foot table and orange divan too much orange-papered wall and foxed window shade, too much café still clinging like the smell of pipe smoke to us in too much wood-plank bed too much stack of café saucer, too much mirror showing mirror showing mirror too much gilt frame, too much sheep-back hunching of bodies all around, too much night street after the café too much plane tree and shadow of plane tree on the cobbled street too much hooded lamp and boulder row of Renault, too much stairway and crystal of bare lightbulbs and shadow down the hall and hard brass doorknobs, all of it too much, all of it with no reason for being there, too much gape of her lips, too much gape of her loins, too much of her and too little of me: I think I'm going to be sick

## SIMONE

one eye dead, one eye drifts away, neither of them looking at me, and I thrash in the vague light on the crumpled sheet not from his touch but from his sightlessness: I have vanished and my invisibility shudders through me like sex and I can hear him thinking inside that wall-eyed head sitting on that tiny body with its tiny parts and he knows me not, but he knows he knows me not, and I know he knows he knows me not, and so I am even more alone in this bed in this room in this shuddering trembling body of mine and I am free

# MILTON BERLE

23, comedian


# AIMEE SEMPLE MCPHERSON

40, evangelist


*in her apartment in Santa Monica, after a Los Angeles charity benefit, 1930*

this is a novelty act on the Orpheum Circuit if there ever was one, the sexy Christian pastor and the good Jewish boy—well not such a good boy, though Mama looks the other way and just packs our bags when I'm hosing down a girl—*I think sex is better than logic, but I can't prove it*—this is more like a freak act, not big enough to close before intermission, this, but maybe we'd go on after the three-spot, presenting the Wandering Youth with the Giant Dong and Sister Aimee with the dust of the Arizona Desert from her phantom kidnapping clinging to her ankles—and pretty ankles they are—*The sex was so good that even the neighbors had a cigarette*— but it's a freak act all right, with the candles burning over there on the dresser and the silver cross and the framed crucifixion— don't look at me, Sister, I didn't do it—*A conscience is what hurts when all your other parts are feeling good*—all that chestnut hair of yours, smelling like the sea—I'd be happy to give your way a try, but *It's hard to be religious when certain people have never been incinerated by a lightning bolt—and you know who you are, you're not laughing right now—what are you, an audience or an oil painting?*—maybe it's just that you know the real me, Sister, you and the silent audience both—forget my baby face, I've been doing this a long time, a long long time already, shtupping and shticking and I'm starting to feel old—*At least I don't drink, I learned that from my Jewish mother, who never touches the stuff, alcohol interferes with her suffering—Jesus may love me, but everybody else thinks I'm a jerk—Sure, there was a time when everybody believed in God, and the Church ruled the world, it was called the Dark Ages—I believe you, Sister, Jesus is coming, but I'm coming first*

## AIMEE

my back bends upward and I can imagine my body turning all the colors, from my toes to the crown of my head, from red to orange to yellow and green and then to blue and indigo and to violet: I am a rainbow, I am a covenant, my Lord *Amen* a covenant *Amen* You put me in this body and the flesh yearns for You and You are the word made flesh and You are also the flesh made word *He shall lie all night betwixt my breasts* and You are present in all your creation, Lord, You are in the sparrow and You are in the beggar by the road and You are in the comedian from the vaudeville stage and with Your infinite tenderness You understood the woman at the well and You understood Your dear Mary Magdalene *Let him kiss me with the kisses of his mouth, for thy love is better than wine* and You understand me, who aches and thrills for You and who cries out Your love, Lord, to the world, for Your gospel is not the gospel of fear and hell and damnation but the gospel of reconciliation and of love, You move in me You fill me up, my Lord, I am full of love for even the least of Your creatures, and this one happens to have a part like the tower of Lebanon which looketh toward Damascus and I hold him close so he can hear the heart in my breast which beats now madly in love of You and he will listen *Amen* and I will soar to You *Amen* and he will believe *Amen* and I say *Amen* and *Amen* and *Amen*

# CLYDE BARROW

25, outlaw

# BONNIE PARKER

23, outlaw

*in a cabin in the woods near Shreveport, Louisiana, on the eve of their death by police ambush, 1934*

some gump I knew wanted to be a tough guy and had no chance, but I was interested in his sister who they said had slipped on the ice and broke her arm and she had it in a sling, and so I go over to the gump's house thinking to make time with the girl now that she's one arm short, and there's noise in the kitchen and I get touchy real fast because they also say the laws is looking for me cause of the little getting-started jobs I've been pulling in McLennan County, and she says *Go on in and meet my friend* and there she is with her back to me, and she turns and the window is behind her and it lights up her strawberry hair like it's a fiery crown and it sure starts to burning in me right away, and the first thing I do after saying my name and she says hers is to reach into my coat pocket and pull out my pistol and lay it on the table that's between us, a 1911-model Colt .45, and this is just to make it clear to her from the first who I am and what she's getting into with me cause it don't take me more than about three seconds with this tiny girl with the red ringlets and the freckles and that smart-aleck half-smile to know she's the one, though I never dream how far she's going to go with me, but the first thing out of my mouth after we get our names and my Colt on the table is *Here is my honest declaration to you, Miss Parker, I am a dangerous man to anybody who gets in the way of me taking what I want and pissing on the shoes of the government that has took every-thing the working stiffs have got, which also means that nobody messes with any woman who is with me* and she moves that half-smile from one side of her mouth to the other, and little did I know that one day I'd give her a .32-caliber Harrington and Richardson top-break pistol for her purse and her eyes would fill with grateful tears

## BONNIE

I hear a noise behind me while I'm standing in Daisy Wickham's kitchen trying to open a jar of Ovaltine at the sink, and my head is full of the darnedest thick mud from the sun coming off the dirty snow outside and from the ticking of a clock and the dripping from the faucet, and I'm sinking fast in that mud cause of this being what my life is—making Ovaltine and hearing these sounds that ask me to just go ahead and beat my head on that window till it cracks—but this noise behind me is footsteps and somehow I know it ain't Daisy, and I turn and there he is with his brown hair slicked back, though a curl of it has figured out how to drop down on his forehead, and his eyes are dark but they might as well be bright red with fire cause they are burning their way into my brain, and he says *I'm Clyde Barrow* and I say *I'm Bonnie Parker* and he pulls a pistol out of his coat and lays it on the table and I don't even for a second worry about a thing 'cause he's giving off something into the air so sweet as to make me want to wiggle my hips, but I keep real still and he says *I mean to be honest with you, Miss Parker, I am a dangerous man but I am a strong man and I can get things for you so that you and me won't ever turn into working stiffs and I can take care of you forever* and I don't know how long forever will be with Clyde Barrow but I am ready to say yes right then

## ADOLF HITLER

46, Reichskanzler and Führer


## INGA ARVAD

22, journalist


*in his office at the Reich Chancellery, during an interview for a Danish newspaper, Berlin, 1935*

pigeons outside the window murmuring at the seed laid out, crumbs in the corners for the mice, Wolf sleeping in the outer office on a leather chair, dreaming—how I wish I could dream his dog's dreams, hanging out of the car with the wind lifting his ears, running fast without even moving his legs—this little mouse beneath me, a perfect Aryan mouse, I will not eat you up, little mouse, I will eat cabbage and lentils and peas instead, not my little mouse, and at my temples I begin to burn and now all my face is burning and I cannot breathe and I cannot sleep and when I do, hands are upon me and my father's whip, my mother's hands and her wild eyes and my face is aflame from what the social democrats have done to us and what the liberals have done and the reactionary monarchists and the capitalists and the communists and the Jews, the Jews, what the Jews have done to us what the Jews have done to all of us and eighty million voices cry out as one and it is for me and they lift their arms and they are inside me, the German people, and they are like a woman, needy, needing, needing, needy beyond thought, needy for strong hands upon them, needy for Fatherland for Father for Empire for the great German Empire needy for Hitler and Hitler will feed the mice and he will kill the beasts how can this be, for soon I stopped taking notes and then I stopped asking questions and I am on the pale plush rug in the middle of his office floor: it was his voice, the unlikely quietness of it, the pain of it, he crossed his hands on his chest and lifted his eyes upward to the ceiling and far beyond, and he was hurt, this man for whom vast throngs of Germans cry out to command them, but for me his eyes lifted in pain and then returned unwavering to me, confiding deeply in me, those eyes came upon me and did not waver and at first they seemed pale blue, a fragile bird's-egg blue, but now they were bright and dark, nearly violet, and these eyes would not move from me and I capped my pen and I trembled at his need and then his voice rose and he began to fill the room with a guttural litany of rage and his crossed arms unfurled and his hands flared and then clenched into fists and leaped up to frame his face and his power filled the room, and even as I trembled in fear I knew that his showing me this was an intimacy, as well: he commanded me fiercely and he needed me desperately, needs me even now, for this brief time, he is strong enough to hold me safe and weak enough for me to hold him safe, and so

# INGA ARVAD

29, journalist

# JOHN F. KENNEDY

24, ensign, U.S. Navy Intelligence

*in room 132, Fort Sumter Hotel, Charleston, South Carolina, February 1942* how can this be, this long skinny boy on his back and it's simple inside that brain of his *Inga Binga hop on let's go* and that was on his mind even as he told me that the FBI is following me and he said he knows I'm not a Nazi spy but Hoover hates the Kennedys and will destroy the number-two son through me but that's okay by him, his big brother Joe can go ahead and be President without him, he's ready to teach history somewhere with his Inga, his Lutheran-former-Miss-Denmark-older-woman-divorcée wife, and to hell with Mama Rose and Papa Joe and he can play touch football with his students, so he said *Inga Binga hop on* and now I let my hair fall into his face and he's always contented for this to be quick, but I won't let him move yet, not this time: his eyes are gray as a winter sky and I'm bundled up in the Tivoli Gardens and there's only the snow and that sky and I'm feeling warm about some toothsome schoolboy and I'm thinking about when the first time will happen and how it will be simple when it does and how there is nothing I need to think about beyond that

## JOHN

young Jack Junior doesn't like to wait standing at attention and if it weren't Inga Binga slowing us down he'd just have to do his business and be done with it, but it's okay since it's her and I'm not sure why, because the world's full of pussies and going after them is like wanting a landslide, getting all the votes, shaking a hand and winning the voter at the other end of it and then the next and the next until every last one of them loves you, but my Inga and her pussy are the whole damn electorate in one, it clasps JJ in its grasp and whispers that it alone is all that counts, and standing now at attention I think perhaps I can be content, I think I can leave the ceaseless striving to the rest of my family, I can give up everything just to be happy like that, but I know how it works, JJ, I'm sorry but I know how it works, when she lets me move—and she soon will—and as soon as you've got what you want, then I'll want to be President again

# J. EDGAR HOOVER

53, Director of the Federal Bureau of Investigation


# CLYDE TOLSON

48, Associate Director


*in Tolson's apartment at the Wardman Park Hotel, Washington, DC,*
*November 1946*

a congressman now, my young Jack, and he will go far and he's all mine, I should have played my favorite of the recordings this afternoon, but it's all right, tomorrow perhaps, and even now I can hear it clearly: the mousy squeaking of the bedsprings as he lies down—on his back, where he will remain, from spinal troubles—and the rustle of his terry-cloth towel being thrown off, he's been walking around the bedroom in a towel after his shower and he never puts his clothes back on with her and he can't wait any longer and he lies down and throws off the towel *Inga Binga hop on let's go* he says and I rewind and I listen to the brief silence after the words, I rewind and it is silent for a few moments, I rewind and he says *Inga Binga hop on let's go* and then I can hear the brief silence of his solitary nakedness, and this time it's not Inga Arvad who approaches his bed but a different woman and he is surprised, but he gives her a close look as she stands before him and he smiles at this new woman, who is older, yes, but she pleasantly evokes a mother figure who nevertheless radiates sensuality, which he desperately needs, and her face is perhaps a bit mannish, but that's appealing too, he likes its sense of command, and he admires her sexy but conservative fluffy black dress with flounces and her feather boa and he says *Hop on* and I do and he is all mine

## CLYDE

in a glass cabinet across the room, our two machine guns—his hanging above mine—from New Orleans and our busting in on Creepy Karpis and his gang, and on the table beside the bed, my weekly orchid—this time he chose a *Cypripedium*, with green and brown speckles on its throat—and he would have led the charge through Creepy's door but for me, but for taking care of his Clyde, holding us back behind the other agents, and when we went in, guns ready, it was shoulder to shoulder, the Director and me, and that night he had Dubonnet carnations delivered to our hotel room and we put them in our button holes and we went out and we ate oysters in the Vieux Carré and the press were popping their bulbs at us, the hero G-men, and little did they know the truth about this great and powerful man, how he was a machine-gun man and he was a flower man and he needed me to hold him

## ALBERT EINSTEIN

66, physicist


## MARGARITA KONENKOVA

51, Soviet spy and wife of Russian expatriate sculptor and fellow
spy Sergei Konenkov


*in Albert's house at 112 Mercer Street, Princeton, New Jersey,*
*July 17, 1945*

## ALBERT

*I lost the office pool* Teller lost the pool and I didn't know if his voice was fuzzy from telephonic static or from grief, and then my dear Margarita arrives moments later and I hope I can do what I have to do—I want to do for her what I have to do—but Teller lost the pool, and so it has happened, the night before the first one went off he said they would put a silver dollar each on the limit of the chain reaction and he said he'd make the uncollectible bet— that there would be no limit, that it would not stop till the earth was incinerated—and if he was right, I would know, and if he was wrong, he would tell me he was wrong so I could know what I am supposed not to know, that it's happened, and we did what we had to do, we have it and Hitler doesn't, but Hitler's done for anyway now and we have it and I am afraid we will find a way to make it useful and I wish I had been a cobbler, I wish what I had to do was be a cobbler; I wish we'd all been cobblers and we had filled the world with shoes

## MARGARITA

he laughs so abruptly sometimes, so ringingly, it's as if all his thoughts have gathered together so hotly and so brilliantly that they explode but it's all right because in the end he finds the universe hilarious, and he walks so distractedly sometimes, dragging the tip of his umbrella along the iron fences of Mercer Street, but if he misses a single picket he stops and returns to touch it, almost tenderly, this Professor Einstein, this Albert, and it all befuddles me, it diverts me from my mission, but I want to get this straight: if the light from a star was our train compartment right now and Albert and I were doing this while moving at the speed of light and if Joe Stalin was watching from far behind us, would we actually be having sex like a truly connected man and woman and it was only old Joe who mistakenly sees Albert in achingly slow motion, not getting it up no matter how hard I try, and sees my eyes slowly filling with tears for not being able to get him really to love me

# RICHARD MILHOUS NIXON

40, Vice President of the United States


# THELMA CATHERINE "PAT" NIXON

41, his wife


*in the bedroom of their home in Washington, DC, 1953*

# RICHARD

Mother was a saint a Quaker saint *I'm ready to go, Mother*, I'm six-teen and as always I rose at four in the terrible dark and I went to Los Angeles and I bought the lettuce and the squash and the snap beans for the grocery and I have returned, with the sun, and I'm ready now to go to school, starched-collared and Windsor-knotted, and I say *Mother I'm ready* and she comes to me and she rises on her toes and she brings her face very near mine and she sniffs, she checks to make sure I am free of halitosis, and she says *Only a faint sweetness* and my breath catches at this, as it always does, I am clean and I will cause no offense and I will succeed on this day and in the night I am caught: I am clutching at myself beneath the sheet and she is standing in the doorway, just come in from closing the store and she's still wearing her coat, a plain cloth coat, a plain Quaker cloth coat, and at her feet our dog pants and slobbers, our cocker spaniel dog, and I am caught and it makes it all the sweeter, I lift my hands from beneath the sheets to show her, I hold them above my head and I say *I am not a masturbator* but I am throbbing on even as I say this and she turns and she goes and she knows and it is sweet and tonight Pat stood in the door in her Republican cloth coat and she brought Checkers, as I had asked, and I was caught and it was very sweet

# PAT

who am I beneath this coat, he did not ask for me to be naked beneath it but I am, I am always naked, beneath a coat, a dress, beneath my smile and the popping of flashbulbs and the clamor of voices, and he is done, my Dick, my Dick is done already in his solitude, the coat is still closed though I am naked beneath it and against my face his breath is faint and abrasive with Listerine and he is silent and I slide my arm beneath him and he does not move and we are young and nothing has begun, we are a young lawyer and a young typing teacher, a couple of amateur actors at the Whittier Community Theatre, and he takes me aside, into the dark of the wings into the smell of mildew and fresh paint and canvas and he says *This is how you make yourself cry* and he teaches me what his college drama coach taught him, to concentrate hard on getting a lump in your throat, and after the lesson he furrows his brow and he clenches his face and makes his lump and he begins to cry, great large tears roll down Dick Nixon's face and beneath them I know he is sad beyond expressing and I wipe at the tears though I know they are fake

## JOSEPH R. MCCARTHY

44, U.S. Senator

## JEAN KERR MCCARTHY

29, his wife and long-time research assistant

*on their honeymoon at Spanish Key in the British West Indies, September 1953*

## JEAN

oh Mama shut up, oh Mama all permed and buttoned tight, oh Mama on your divan covered in vinyl to keep the flower upholstery pristine and unsoiled and untouched, oh Mama your voice fills the gathering dimness of your living room, the low-watt bulbs turned off until the light of day has vanished utterly, oh Mama shut up, stop your last-minute warnings, thinking I'm still a virgin, stop your talk of sex and the male conspiracy of it, its infiltration, its invasion, he is heavy on me yes, he is heavy as you said, yes, but shut up Mama, he is sweating yes and I want to rub it off my face and shoulders with the back of my wrist, hard, yes, but shut up, Mama, I am married to him and he is a great man and he will save our country but I cannot even look at him in this moment while I'm hearing your voice, Mama, so I turn my face away from him for now and I say to you *Mama, please shut the hell up* her eyes just moved, she should be looking at me and only at me but her eyes shifted to the left, off the bed, and she has put facts in my head and words in my mouth plenty these past few years of the crusade and she has felt my wrath and tasted my kisses and so she should know better than to take her eyes off me in the middle of me plucking her chicken, churning her butter, plowing her field with a blunt blade, so there is a reason to watch when her eyes shift off the bed at a time like this and I should stop and see what's up but things just keep going on even though it could be that she heard a faint scuff of footsteps outside the door or a rasp of a pass key in the lock, someone ready to bust in blazing away with their Kalashnikov AK-47 automatic weapons, whose development and manufacture were financed secretly by the March of Dimes, thanks to Franklin Roosevelt, whose own eyes shifted away from the cameras at Yalta to give Joe Stalin a wink, and she's still looking away and maybe the enemy is already in the room, maybe the enemy is right beneath us, under the bed, waiting, maybe my wife herself is one of them, maybe there's a man under our bed and she's just waiting for me to be done and waiting for me to fall asleep and then she will tap twice lightly on the mattress and he will come up and he will slide in beside her and he will whisper to her in a language I do not understand

# ROBERT F. KENNEDY

36, Attorney General of the United States


# MARILYN MONROE

35, actress


*in the Santa Monica beach house of Kennedy's brother-in-law, Peter Lawford, 1962*

## ROBERT

my high hectoring whine let you be cool and calm and I elected
you, and I keep your secrets secret—your back and your pain-
killers and your women—and they love you, the women, even
when they're being hustled away five minutes later with that
dazed flutter in their eyes from it being over so quick, and in a
foggy February morning off the coast of Maine I leap into the
waves and you dare not follow and the cold nearly stops my heart
but I do not care: I am gaunt and I brood and my eyes goggle
slightly more than yours—the difference between handsome and
creepy—and I was Runt to the old man and I was Little Bobby
the Devout to Mother and I am Black Robert to you and—mea
culpa, mea maxima culpa—I am with this woman, and it's true I
am with her only after you, only because of you, but to her I am
The General and I am at ten minutes and counting and I dare
not ask but I can hear her saying inside her head *Oh, General, yes
yes you are ever so much better in bed than the President*

## MARILYN

nothing but the slowing of my heart, nothing but filling up in the hungry place, and the hunger stops at once as if it was nothing to start with, but the fullness inside that part of me makes another kind of nothing and I float with that, I can turn my head as I float and I can feel my face moving, my eyes falling on something—a clock on a blond wood chest of drawers—and I feel my face turn again and the ceiling is spackled and the nothing that is usually trying to claw its way out of my chest, out of my wrists, out of my throat and eyes and brain, the nothing that I am, the nothing worth anything: that nothing is gone and the nothing that remains is some man, a man of a certain bulk, of a certain scent, of a certain murmuring, a certain sighing, a certain panting and wanting and wanting—wanting me—and to me it is nothing, but the nothing it pours into me lets me close my eyes and rest a few moments from what I am

# WILLIAM JEFFERSON CLINTON

24, law student


# HILLARY DIANE RODHAM

23, law student


*in his second-floor bedroom at a rented beach house in Milford, Connecticut, late spring, 1971*

this had to be done eventually and the personal is political all right and if your underwear and your armpits and your hairdo and your shoes are political then choosing to fuck a specific man in a specific bed on a specific day is political and it's merely political and he's the one all right because everything we talk about makes it clear: McGovern next year and somebody after that and somebody after that and somebody after that and then he and I may choose to fuck in Lincoln's bed or on the eagle on the floor in the Oval Office, and I don't care if that's the next time we do this, to be honest with myself, but I choose this time and I will choose some others in between because one day we'll be fucking on the eagle and there's a soft knock at the door and the secretary knows not to barge in and she says *Madame President, the Soviet premier is on the phone*

## BILL

this has to be done at this point, though I miss the surprise, I miss the gasp from a grab of their tits or the dropping of my pants when they least expect it, but there are plenty of others for that, this one's not in her body yet, which is cute enough in spite of her severe qualms, but at least I did get her to shave her legs pretty quick and I can sometimes surprise her into a brief silence with some line of reasoning—McGovern's chances for the nomination or Ping-Pong as metaphor for Chinese-American relations or some other thing that comes to my lips as quick as kisses—and I did at least rip those red-frame glasses off her face, and Coltrane is playing in my head—*A Love Supreme*—and my lips go itchy and not for Hillary's mouth on mine but for an abandoned ambition, me on the sax forever, though the twinge passes quickly now because Coltrane's power is detached from his own moment-to-moment life, even in the clubs, the ones he's got hold of are out beyond the glare of lights, beyond his direct touch, I was right to let that go, let go of being a surgeon, too, where you exercise your ultimate power only when they don't even know it from the anesthetics, I know the path for me and this girl knows it too, better than anybody else—I can see crowds, great large crowds to wade into and to touch—she's smart and she's tough and I know she won't put up with certain things from me and I don't want to lose her but before she's done here I've got to figure out how to get on top

# ELVIS PRESLEY

42, singer


# HOLLY SINGLETON

20, admirer


*in his dressing room at the Market Square Arena, Indianapolis, Indiana, after what would be his last public performance, June 26, 1977*

he was singing all in white in this kind of jumpsuit with a big golden something on him, like the sun, but it was split in half by his bare chest and it was about driving me crazy to see that, and now listen to me, I'm naked with him and I should be memorizing his body but instead I'm trying to remember him from the stage even though he's right here with me in his own private dressing room and he's touching me and I can look at what I've always dreamed about seeing but I can't stop *thinking* about seeing him instead of actually opening my darn eyes and *seeing*, like what if you had ten minutes with Jesus and you kept thinking *Wow here I am with Jesus, Wow God's Chosen Son is sitting right in front of me* instead of going *Jesus, is it okay to use my tongue when I kiss my boyfriend* and *Please Jesus, my mama's about driving me crazy with her criticism, is it dishonoring her to tell her to stop even if I don't actually say "shut up"* and look what I'm doing now, I'm thinking about talking to Jesus when *Elvis* is right here, and my head is so full of stupid thoughts that I'm not even seeing him, and even thinking about how my thoughts are stupid is stupid because it's still more of not seeing him, but really, if I do see him, if I do actually look at Elvis Presley's naked body, how will I ever go on with the rest of my life

you're how it used to be, pretty lady, me singing like it's just for some new girl in the front row, but all this goes way back, Mama and me sitting in chairs in the little patch of grass at the Lauderdale Courts and she's been waiting up for me and she's past being mad, she knows I been on Beale Street, at dusk I went on and walked out of Pinchgut and down Lauderdale to Beale, and like I do, I'm moving from door to door at the clubs, listening, and somewhere along the way somebody who knew to see me finally says *Let that white boy in* and I go in trembling and it's Arthur Crudup singing and he is singing to me and he is singing about me, this colored man with his dark angel voice who knows every pain in the world, and I come back and before Mama can say anything I sit down alongside her, and behind us and above us there's voices shouting at each other and there's a dog barking somewhere and there's a woman's crying, too, coming from a window and a boat whistle from the river and I lean to Mama and I touch her arm, and this is just for her, and though I'm feeling already that some-day I'll do this for everybody and I'll do it with a beat and I'll move my body to the life of it, for now I sing just to her, real soft and slow *That's all right now, Mama, anyway you do*

## DIANA

25, Princess of Wales

## CHARLES PHILIP ARTHUR GEORGE

37, Prince of Wales and Earl of Chester, Duke of Cornwall, Duke
of Rothesay, Earl of Carrick and Baron of Renfrew, Lord of the
Isles, Prince and Great Steward of Scotland, heir apparent to the
British throne

*at King Juan Carlos's Marivent Palace near Palma, Majorca,
August 1986, for the last time*

now that he's begun this and is humphing softly in confusion,
trying to work out just why he's even trying, I need to breathe
deep and curl my toes on the edge of the pool at Park House and
there's a smell of the salt sea in the air and there are yew trees
and silver birch and pine all around and I saw a young fox in the
morning and he and I stood on the lawn and looked at each other
for a long long while and I stand now waiting for just the right
moment to dive, my arms outstretched, bending over the water at
the deep end, and all my dolls have been properly walked in their
pram and all the animals on my bed have been stroked and put
just so and Daddy is puttering in the garden and my sisters are
lounging in the sunlight and my brother is napping inside and
Mummy hasn't legged it yet—I don't even know it's coming—so I
wait at the edge of the pool for just the right moment and I don't
understand that it would be ever so advisable just to plunge on in
and glide to the bottom and not come back up at all, not at all, for
it will never be anywhere near as nice as this again, ever

## CHARLES

Uncle Dickie, how can I disagree with you, and Mum, you are the paragon of Uncle Dickie's advice are you not, how unsettled one should be if another man has touched your wife before you have found her, how disturbing for her sweet-charactered allure, for her fresh-budded tenderness to have been known fully by another man who shall then carry around forever the intimate memory of the King's wife in his mind to take out and fondle and treasure as if it were all still his, and so she is thus, my wife, but she is gaunt from her virginity, she is chlorine and ammonia and antiseptic, and of course she weeps and faints and has no sense of me because there is no sense in her of any other life, no sense of any other man by which to measure me, to give meaning to any loving word she would say to me: she is slick and untouched as a fish and I would cling to a horse who's been ridden

## ROOSTER

2, stud


## CHICKEN

1, roaster



*in a barnyard in Alabama, 2000*

# ROOSTER

they used to look at me different, the sweet chicks—I know that
much—not so detached, not so stupid, but they didn't used to have
wings and feathers, either—I peck at little bits of that previous
life I must have lived like pecking at yummy pieces of overlooked
corn out in the midst of the grit and pebbles oh boy, and now I'm
on her and oh boy oh boy, and yes the chicks used to be—how did
I stand it?—utterly featherless, utterly, and they used to look at
me with pleading awe and wonder, which was a better look—why
the difference now?—I was rich then, oh yes, and I had splen-
did plumage, I'm sure, great red hackles and a tall comb, I was a
magnificent looking something or other, a cock, a cocksman—oh
ruffle and strut oh ruffle and strut and hop on and I am really
something right now and I'm fucking and clucking and she's
loving it like crazy because I am the man around here, and over
there beyond the fence are the featherless ones, who, in spite of
their puny plumage—or perhaps because of it—seem very familiar to me, and suddenly I understand: they are watching me and
they are listening to me cluck and they are laughing at the sounds
I make that they don't understand, but I know that someday they
will be sweet little chicks, too, and I'll be waiting for them

## CHICKEN

eggy eggy eggy and then the little fluffs will come out and I will hover and fluff up too and they will huddle beneath me and this is a very useful cock I think, he flares his tail and puffs up his hackles very nice and he struts very nice and sometimes I wonder what that's all about why I am impressed with that and then I wonder what is this farm thing going on and then it's like, whoa, was that a stop sign I blew through, and there's a big commotion all around me and I think I better call my agent, and then I go, like, what's a stop sign? what's an agent? and just as I am about to answer myself, the thoughts are gone—these moments of confusion don't come so often anymore—I just wish this dude would get it over with because I've got a lot of pecking in the dirt to do, like it's all I can do to score some corn around here

## KEVIN SMITH

32, advertising copywriter

## JULIA HANSON SMITH

30, graphic designer

*in their apartment in Brooklyn, the night of September 11, 2001*

## KEVIN

I know the night is filled with smoke and with fire and I would not have thought it would be my wife clinging to me now because of what I have done: I should have gone out the door last night after my clumsiness, she was half-turned at the stove, the steam rising before her from the boiling rice, and all that I'd planned carefully to say came out impulsively, simply, badly, *I am in love* and she knew it was not her and she laid the lid on the pot and she turned her back to me and later we sat in chairs in the dark of our living room for a long while, the pot charred black on the stove, and I did not go and then it was this morning and then the long day and I am in love and I think it is not with her, but tonight, in this moment, we dare not change a thing

## JULIA

how can it be so quiet from across the river, if you do not make yourself look you might never realize the terrible thing going on, and he and I do not look, we know but we choose for this night not to look, even into our own hearts, though I can hear faintly through the wall someone weeping and from another place the murmur of television voices, and I see myself standing in an open window high above the city: I cannot go back inside and I cannot step into the empty air, and from this distance I am only a figure standing in a window, I can only try to imagine what I am feeling

## GEORGE W. BUSH

57, President of the United States

## LAURA BUSH

57, First Lady

*in the master bedroom of the White House, March 2004*

## LAURA

the Nancy Reagan wallpaper here is very nice, actually—all the
peacocks and roosters and bluebirds hand-painted on Chinese
paper—she was a good strong Republican woman—is that my
cell phone?—no, just a ringing in my ears—I'll have to hold my
nostrils and blow when I get a chance, which won't be long—
wallpaper, wallpaper—I'm not sure about the wallpaper design
in the Lincoln Bedroom, but that pallid lemon stuff will go
and also the carpet, with those flowers so pale they look dead—
a diamond-grid English Wilton's the thing for the floor, bold
Victorian greens and purples and yellows like the sunlight—and
a new mattress for the bed, though I better not let Mother Bush
know or she'll have one of her conniptions, since it was she who
finally replaced the horsehair, but her mattress is lumpy and
always was—everybody says so, including Jeb—and it has to go—
and I guess I'll leave the Lincoln Bathroom alone for now, it has
a quaint Fifties air about it and it'll make George happy to keep it
the same—he does have his own sense of history, with his project
of peeing in all thirty-five of the White House bathrooms and he
wants them to be just like they've always been

## GEORGE

so I should have said to Pretty Boy from the National Public Radio today that I meant what I said when I said *the tar on wearer* instead of *the war on terror* 'cause I had on my new boots down in Crawford, see, and the county was resurfacing Mill Road and I got tar on those boots, walking along, so I said what I meant and I meant what I said: I regret the necessity to have tar on the wearer but you got to walk on the road to get someplace in Iraq 'cause over there they die with their boots on, I should have said that and Pretty Boy would've just scratched his pointy head and I'd've given him my special little knowing smile which I have given to plenty of these pencilheads and they don't even have a clue what that smile means, which is when I'm out of office I'll have each of you that got that smile down to Crawford, one at a time, and you think it's to get a story about the doofus back on his ranch, but when you get there, I'll make you a proposition, each one of you, which is: admit it, you've dreamed about punching me in the nose, you figure I ain't so tough without my Presidential war powers and you figure I'm plenty stupid and you'd like to whip my ass, well now's your chance, just real private, we'll go out to the clearing by Rainey Creek and take off our jackets and we will have it out like real men and I will kick your ass unremitt-lessly till you're crying for your white-haired little old mama even though she slapped you around pretty good when you were a boy 'cause that's who you're dealing with. Not the mama. The guy who can whip your ass

## ROBERT OLEN BUTLER

62, writer, Vietnam veteran

## MISS X

36, hotel desk clerk, daughter of North Vietnamese soldier

*in room 1503, Sheraton Saigon Hotel and Towers, August 11, 2007*

## ROBERT

we washed with Sheraton soap, a Coca-Cola on the night table, CNN muted on the TV screen, the new Saigon outside, fifteen stories below, the motorcycle roar barely audible over the AC fan, she'd reached her hand around her computer and across the registration desk to touch my wrist, an impossibly awkward gesture as if to say *Here is your past in this place, determined to touch you*, and I said *Em đẹp như nàng tiên—you are beautiful as a fairy princess*, an old-fashioned compliment she'd never heard from any man, much less an American—and then later she was at my door and we touched lips and we held each other and she whispered softly *Trời ơi*, a summoning of God, but familiarly, as if God were a lover passing unaware on the other side of the street, and now as we hold even closer to each other there is a sudden quieting in me: *trời ơi*, since I was first in this city, thirty-six years, four wives, a father, a hundred thousand special moments of the body, my Saigon have all passed: let me kiss her again now, for I am distracted, and I do, and a woman's lips move against mine speaking their own secret language, which, after all the years of my life, I still yearn to understand

## MISS X

all I have of him are some photos the size of my palm, my father, he smiles into the sunlight that half closes his eyes, he smiles for the daughter he will never see, and I have a flag, red with a yellow star, carefully folded, and I have stories of his bravery for his country, and there is a certain kind of ghost who comes with irony, who comes in an unexpected form to whisper that it is all right to laugh and to be in a body for a while, and this man I hold now called me something a man would call his daughter and I believe his smile and his hands and I am not yet a ghost so I touched him to begin and I touch him some more and he speaks in a father's voice and I will hold him even closer though once he could have pulled the trigger himself

# KEVIN SMITH

38, advertising executive

# JULIA HANSON

36, art gallery manager

*in her Manhattan apartment, October 16, 2007*

our words—only an hour ago, in a coffee shop in the West Village, each of us alone at a table, and then an accidental synchronicity of glances over the *Times* and then her hesitation—for it was her decision to make—and then her yes, I'll rise and come to you—our words still run through my head like reefer smoke, smoothing things over, blurring what our bodies remembered of the last time *You look good* I said *So do you* she said *Are you still* she began and I interrupted *No* I said too sharply and I knew she wanted more and I said *Another man* and she laughed, but gently, *Perhaps it was with the man who just left me* she said and we looked into each other's eyes and we knew we were both burned down, we were both rubble, and I move now inside her and she splays her hands hard on my back and when we are done, when I can find my breath, my voice, I will say I'm sorry

## JULIA

a thing that was gone all this time, a small thing, now that it has returned I understand how badly I missed it, the thumb edge of his right hand, how as he begins to move inside me he always strokes my hair with that edge of his hand, for a long while, and I turn my face a little in that direction I want to kiss his hand and I imagine these past few years unwinding—I unweep, I unpretend I am in love, I undeceive myself, I unfuck, I unmeet a man I force myself to care for, and I go all the way back to us, to my husband and me, we undivorce, we unfall, we unburn, the world we knew unchanges—but this is a small thing, his familiar hand upon my hair, and I know that even on a bright clear morning something terrible can fly in your window, but until then I will kiss his hand and we will try once more

## SANTA CLAUS

471, philanthropist


## INGEBIRGITTA

826, elf


*in a back room of Santa's workshop, North Pole, January 2008*

## SANTA

well well well ho ho ho I am a naughty boy no doubt about it, but she understands, my overstuffed Christmas turkey of a Mrs. Claus, with her hair bunned up tight, the color of Stockholm street slush, and I'm happy to put a lump of coal in my own stocking for the sake of this sweet elf's hair unfurled and floating all about us, filling the room, covering us over, the undulant red of the bottom fringe of an auroral curtain *At least she's an older woman* my plump pudding of a Mrs. Claus says, and it's sad really how she can take comfort from that technicality, for this is our two hundred fifty-second January, my elf and I, and she still looks as young as Barbie, and after my wild night of plunging into chimneys and clothes-drier vents and pussy-cat doors and keyholes I must—even if only from the sympathetic magic of it—fly through the dark passage of my elf and give her gifts *You need to unwind* my bloated-to-bursting goose of a Mrs. Claus says *I'll just bake some cookies* and I am dashing and dancing and cometing and vixening but my Christmas wish once again is that I could just do this and stop thinking about my wife

## INGEBIRGITTA

he's been in too many human houses: he is so like them now, he is so distracted, he is indeed so like a bowl full of jelly, where has my good Father Christmas gone, before he got this jolly image and before he got his livestock and his fan mail and his four million Google hits—twice as many as the Easter Bunny, he loves to say—but if only you knew, my dear, how often I think I'd prefer the bunny—though you are a kindly one and you are a merry one and you are a droll one, these are trivial things to me, I am an elf, I am of forest duff and I am of tree-bark dew and I am of quaking top-leaves and I am always of this trembling yearning body and I can dance a man to death, but you are managed now and you are spun and, worst of all, you think too much, and all I really want from you, dear Santa, is a Dirty Decadence 12-Speed Rabbit-Wand Double-Dip Flex-O-Pulse Vibrator

# THE
# COUPLES

ADAM, 7, first man
EVE, 7, first woman
*the first day after the new moon of the fourth month of the eighth year after Creation*

ZEUS, 982, King of the Gods
LEDA, 20, Queen of Sparta
*1215 BC*

HELEN, 25, Queen of Sparta, wife of Menelaus
PARIS, 22, Prince of Troy
*1194 BC*

HELEN, 35, Princess of Troy
MENELAUS, 42, King of Sparta
*1184 BC*

MARY MAGDALENE, 24, prostitute
TIBERIUS AURELIUS GAVROS, 22, Roman soldier
*AD 28*

CLEOPATRA VII, 28, Queen of Egypt
MARCUS ANTONIUS, 42, member of Rome's ruling triumvirate
*AD 41*

ATTILA, 47, Khan of the Huns
ILDICO, 17, his twelfth wife
*AD 453*

IZUMI SHIKIBU, 29, lady of the court
PRINCE ATSUMICHI, 31, husband of Princess Atsumichi
*1003*

LUCREZIA BORGIA, 21, daughter of Pope Alexander VI, Rodrigo Borgia
ALFONSO D'ESTE, 25, her husband, eldest son of the Duke of Ferrara
*1502*

HENRY VIII, 44, King of England
ANNE BOLEYN, 34, Queen of England
*1535*

WILLIAM SHAKESPEARE, 29, poet and playwright
HENRY WRIOTHESLEY, THIRD EARL OF SOUTHAMPTON, 20, courtier
and literary patron
*1593*

COTTON MATHER, 56, clergyman and author
LYDIA LEE MATHER, 45, his third wife
*1719*

WOLFGANG AMADEUS MOZART, 31, composer
NANCY STORACE, 21, soprano
*1787*

LOUIS XVI, 23, King of France
Maria Antonia Josefa Johanna von Habsburg-Lothringen, known in France as
MARIE ANTOINETTE, 21, Queen of France
*1777*

THOMAS JEFFERSON, 45, U.S. Ambassador to France
SALLY HEMINGS, 16, slave, half-sister to Jefferson's dead wife
*1788*

NAPOLÉON BONAPARTE, 26, general in command of the French
"Army of Italy"
JOSÉPHINE DE BEAUHARNAIS, 33, his wife
FORTUNÉ, 4, her dog
*1796*

BENJAMIN, 23, field slave
HANNAH, 17, house slave
*1855*

JOHN WILKES BOOTH, 24, actor
CATHERINE WINSLOW, 26, actress
*1863*

ABRAHAM LINCOLN, 54, President of the United States
MARY TODD LINCOLN, 44, First Lady
*1863*

MARTHA JANE "CALAMITY JANE" CANARY, 24, frontierswoman
JAMES BUTLER "WILD BILL" HICKOK, 39, gambler and gunfighter
*1876*

WALT WHITMAN, 64, poet
OSCAR WILDE, 28, poet and playwright
*1883*

SIGMUND FREUD, 42, psychiatrist
MINNA BERNAYS, 33, his sister-in-law
*1898*

LIZZIE ANDREW BORDEN, 44, acquitted murderer
NANCE O'NEIL, 30, actress
*1904*

JAMES JOYCE, 24, writer
NORA BARNACLE, 22, his wife
*1906*

PABLO PICASSO, 24, artist
FERNANDE OLIVIER, 25, model
*1906*

GERTRUDE STEIN, 36, writer
ALICE B. TOKLAS, 33, her companion
*1910*

VICTOR DE SATODE PEÑASCO Y CASTELLANA, 18, of independent
means from Madrid
MARIA JOSEFA PEREDEZE SOTO Y VALLEJO
PEÑASCO Y CASTELLANA, 17, his newly wed wife
*1912*

MATA HARI, 37, exotic dancer and courtesan
JACK JOHNSON, 35, world heavyweight boxing champion
*1913*

GEORGE HERMAN "BABE" RUTH, 21, baseball player
JOSEPHINE RUGGLES, 24, prostitute
*1916*

ERNEST HEMINGWAY, 23, writer
CÉLINE GAUTHIER, 34, prostitute
*1922*

JOSEPHINE BAKER, 19, dancer
GEORGES SIMENON, 22, writer
*1926*

JEAN-PAUL SARTRE, 24, recent graduate in philosophy from
the École Normale Supérieure
SIMONE DE BEAUVOIR, 21, recent graduate in philosophy
from the Sorbonne
*1929*

MILTON BERLE, 23, comedian
AIMEE SEMPLE MCPHERSON, 40, evangelist
*1930*

CLYDE BARROW, 25, outlaw
BONNIE PARKER, 23, outlaw
*1934*

ADOLF HITLER, 46, Reichskanzler and Führer
INGA ARVAD, 22, journalist
*1935*

INGA ARVAD, 29, journalist
JOHN F. KENNEDY, 24, ensign, U.S. Navy Intelligence
*1942*

J. EDGAR HOOVER, 53, Director of the Federal Bureau of Investigation
CLYDE TOLSON, 48, Associate Director
*1946*

ALBERT EINSTEIN, 66, physicist
MARGARITA KONENKOVA, 51, Soviet spy
*1945*

RICHARD MILHOUS NIXON, 40, Vice President of the United States
THELMA CATHERINE "PAT" NIXON, 41, his wife
*1953*

JOSEPH R. MCCARTHY, 44, U.S. Senator
JEAN KERR MCCARTHY, 29, his wife
*1953*

ROBERT F. KENNEDY, 36, Attorney General of the United States
MARILYN MONROE, 35, actress
*1962*

WILLIAM JEFFERSON CLINTON, 24, law student
HILLARY DIANE RODHAM, 23, law student
*1971*

ELVIS PRESLEY, 42, singer
HOLLY SINGLETON, 20, admirer
*1977*

DIANA, 25, Princess of Wales
CHARLES PHILIP ARTHUR GEORGE, 37, Prince of Wales and Earl
of Chester, Duke of Cornwall, Duke of Rothesay, Earl of Carrick and Baron
of Renfrew, Lord of the Isles, Prince and Great Steward of Scotland, heir
apparent to the British throne
*1986*

ROOSTER, 2, stud
CHICKEN, 1, roaster
*2000*

KEVIN SMITH, 32, advertising copywriter
JULIA HANSON SMITH, 30, graphic designer
*2001*

GEORGE W. BUSH, 57, President of the United States
LAURA BUSH, 57, First Lady
*2004*

ROBERT OLEN BUTLER, 62, writer
MISS X, 36, hotel desk clerk
*2007*

KEVIN SMITH, 38, advertising executive
JULIA HANSON, 36, art gallery manager
*2007*

SANTA CLAUS, 471, philanthropist
INGEBIRGITTA, 826, elf
*2008*